SHADOW'S WATCH

SHADOW ISLAND SERIES: BOOK FIVE

MARY STONE

LORI RHODES

D1737149

DESCRIPTION

The shadows are watching...

Less than twenty-four hours after Hurricane Boris ravages Shadow Island, it delivers one final blow. Two corpses, lashed together, wash up on the shore. Some of them, anyway.

With no primary crime scene, no witnesses, and barely any human remains, Sheriff Rebecca West has precious little to work with. Are these victims connected to the seemingly untouchable Yacht Club, or did Boris's awesome power simply push them onto her beach?

When the investigation identifies one of the John Does as a well-liked skipper who lived and worked a hundred miles away, Rebecca has more questions than answers. Was he simply at the wrong place at the wrong time? And who is the second victim? And why were his fingers chopped off before he was tossed into the sea?

When another body turns up on the beach with its fingers also missing, Rebecca knows one thing for certain. Boris might have swept the first victims onto her little island, but a murderer had already been waiting...and watching...there.

From its ghastly beginning to the unexpected final chapter, Shadow's Watch—the fifth book in the Shadow Island Series by Mary Stone and Lori Rhodes—will make you question how well you really know the people in your life.

1

———————

S kipper sat on the deck of his boat and stared out at the vast and ever-changing blues of the tranquil sea and cloudless sky. On a typical morning, this would have been precisely what he'd need to calm his mind. To sit and take in the beautiful day.

Today, though, his mind was anything but calm.

Today is when I die.

A storm was raging around him, and it had nothing to do with the weather or even the sea. There had been no sign, no radar signal, no change in pressure to warn him. It was almost funny. People talked about how tempestuous the sea was or how dangerous the creatures swimming below its surface could be. But Skipper knew humans and their unpredictably explosive natures were the deadliest forces of all.

Especially the human onboard his boat right then.

Jerking against the braided nylon binding his wrists behind him, Skipper mentally cursed when the rope didn't give. Red, his buddy, was tied to his back in a similar manner, while a crazed man cycloned up and down the deck. Trying again, he twisted his wrists to work a bit of slack, but the effort caused the woven cord to bite into his flesh.

It was painful, but he knew it was possible to stretch the rope slightly if he kept working to unwind the intertwined threads. He stopped when his fingers brushed against something thick and wet with a hard center—a rib?—and the man at his back screamed.

He wanted to tell Red to keep quiet but he knew his cry had been involuntary.

Skipper lowered his voice and twisted his head to be close to his friend's ear. "I'm trying to work my hands loose. I'm sorry if I'm hurting you. Please hang in there."

There was no answer except for pained sobbing. Skipper's heart broke for him.

Dammit! Even if it hurts, it's better than what will happen if I don't get us free.

In more than sixty years of life, Skipper had never been in a situation this bad. He was sitting in a puddle of blood and saltwater in the middle of a tarp spread out underneath them. Most of the blood wasn't his, which somehow made it much worse. The sticky tackiness drying on his pants as the warming sun climbed in the sky made him squirm on the plastic sheet, making a squishing sound with every movement.

He'd been able to stand from a cross-legged seated position in his youth, but there was no way he could manage that now with his bad knees. It didn't matter anyway, since he would never manage to get to his feet in the right position with his buddy lashed to his back. Of course, if he were still in his prime, he wouldn't have been jumped so easily, and maybe they could have fought off their attacker instead of being knocked down by the first, unexpected blow.

The pirate, as good a name as any for a madman who hijacked his boat, had taught him what attempted escape

2

———

Looking through the windshield at the tattered beach, Sheriff Rebecca West took a moment for herself. The island had just weathered a major hurricane less than twenty-four hours ago, and she'd only just returned home after sheltering at the health center.

She was supposed to have the day off. In some parallel universe, where a hurricane hadn't rocked the island and dead bodies weren't surfacing at random, she'd imagined spending it with Ryker Sawyer. There was definitely more than friendship between them, but timing never seemed to quite work to their advantage. Instead of enjoying Ryker's company, she'd been called out to a crime scene, and it was barely nine a.m.

The level of destruction that Hurricane Boris had caused was heart-wrenching. Although, driving into town, she realized that despite the amplitude of residue from the ocean left everywhere, it was so much worse at the edge of the sea.

In the hours since the hurricane had made landfall, the barometric pressure had returned almost to normal, and the would result in. Several quick, hard blows had put an end to that. Skipper licked his split lip and spat the blood out.

Here he was in the middle of nowhere. He hadn't been allowed to consult any of his charts, but he reckoned they were in international waters. They weren't even near a shipping lane. Skipper would need to find his own way out of this predicament.

Their pirate was still pacing from bow to stern, passing them as he ranted and raved, using mostly obscenities. It might have even been funny, if not for the murderous look and his casual use of violence.

"How could you be so stupid? All you had to do was follow instructions and keep your mouth shut." The pirate punched Red. Again.

Skipper lurched forward with his head snapping down before he registered Red's grunt. Every blow jarred through Skipper's back.

"Why would you do something so idiotic? What were you thinking?"

"C'mon, man, leave off. He told you already!" There wasn't much Skipper could do to stop the intruder, but he couldn't just sit there and let his buddy get pummeled to death.

"I told you. I…I didn't have a choice." Red's response was weak and desperate. "He needed to know about you being—"

Skipper felt Red stiffen before another blow rocked them both.

The pirate stomped off again. "Of course you had a choice! You told my secret. You stole from me. Who forced you to do either?"

The headache came almost instantly with a dull throbbing pain behind Skipper's ear. He continued to wiggle his wrists while the pirate was distracted.

Red found a bit of strength. "I had to think of my family! Of myself! I couldn't just—"

The pirate's feet pounded across the deck, and a loud slap cut off Red's words. Again, both men rocked.

"You should have been thinking about what I'd do when I found out you were lying and stealing, you little piece of shit."

"Please, please! I can fix this. I can."

The pirate loomed over them. "How?"

Skipper prayed his friend had a way to get them both out of this.

He hadn't done anything wrong. His predicament could be chalked up to being in the wrong place at the wrong time. It was easy to accept that when it came to storms or choppy seas, but that was something Skipper could navigate through. Now he was stuck, depending on someone else to keep him alive.

Before Red could respond, a terrible *thunk* of metal meeting flesh lurched Skipper forward. Skipper prayed with more force than he ever had. But as a fresh gush of warm blood flowed under him, he knew something irrevocable had just happened.

With one final, guttural cry, Red pitched forward, his deadweight dragging Skipper backward and arching his back, leaving him more exposed to what might come next.

Holy Mary...er, God...Savior. Filled with despair, Skipper tried to remember the prayers from his youth but couldn't. *Pray for this sinner. Or me. Dammit, I know I'm not supposed to swear in a prayer. Please, just get me out of this alive, and I promise I'll be a better man.*

He knew if he survived this, he would have nightmares for the rest of his life. Nightmares he would welcome over the alternative. He wanted to scream, but he felt a vibration on his back. Groaning? Was Red still alive? He went silent and focused.

Nothing.

After several moments, he lowered himself back onto his rear before daring to peek over his shoulder toward the pirate.

The shadow of the man cast over them. Something long was in his hand—the gaff!

By the time the massive hook registered in Skipper's mind, the business end was already swinging downward. With a reflexive surge of adrenaline, he snapped his head down to duck out of the way, using his friend as an unintended shield.

There was a sickening *crunch*. Red's body swayed but didn't jerk as the second and third blows fell.

A scream rose in Skipper's throat when he realized his friend was dead for sure. What did this mean for him now?

He clamped his fingers on the severed stubs where Red's fingers had once been, hoping he was wrong. There was no reaction. He squeezed again, hoping for a scream, a jerk, a cry, anything to indicate he was still breathing.

Nothing.

Shit.

Skipper could barely hear the mumbled words of the pirate, who'd resumed pacing. "I didn't want to do this. I didn't want any of this. Why did he have to be such a dumbass?"

There was no one left to help Skipper. No one else was on the boat. Just him and the murderer.

Trying to think of anything he could say to get himself out of this situation, Skipper looked around. He knew this boat like the back of his hand, having spent a third of his life on the deck. There was nothing nearby he could use, even if he could have reached for it. He always kept a clean deck.

Everything was tucked away so no one would trip and accidentally hurt themselves. How ironic that his own safety precautions might now contribute to his demise.

The stretch of placid ocean mocked him and reminded him that screaming for help would be fruitless and even embarrassing. Out in the middle of the sea, there really was nothing. No law, no help, no hope, no—

That gave him an idea.

"You don't have to do anything else."

The pacing stopped. "What did you say?"

Skipper lifted his eyes, the shadow frozen in place over his shoulder. The man was huge and ripped for someone his age.

"You killed him because of what he did. That's all done now. No one saw what happened out here. I'm sure as hell not going to tell anyone. There are no records. No one saw us leave port. Your mission is complete." He gulped, praying he sounded convincing.

When there was no response, he pressed on. "Red did you wrong. He screwed up. He paid for it. A simple matter of making things right. You could even call it justice. Now it's all said and done, and we can go back to our lives. Things happen at sea all the time, and no one can do anything about it."

He kept his eyes on the ominous shadow, praying he'd gotten through.

"Go back?" The shadow shook his head. "There's no going back."

"Of course we can. You've got all the power out here. You make the decisions. If you decide that enough is enough, we can just…go. But you'll need someone to captain the ship to get you back."

"All the power?" He laughed, and it was a terrible noise.

Skipper heard death in that laugh as surely as he could feel it resting against his back. "Yes."

"This wasn't about power. This was about trust." There was a slithering sound that Skipper knew all too well. The tarp was being folded. "And, unlike you two, I'm not going to end up as fish food."

The man flipped the tarp over them, blinding Skipper to his surroundings. The light turned blue around him as he tried to twist free while kicking at the tarp.

The world grew bluer as another layer of tarp was thrown over him and his dead friend. With all the plastic bound up over his head, his buddy's blood pooled around him more thickly.

Skipper's stomach turned, and he prayed he wouldn't throw up on top of everything else.

Seems like the least of your worries, ya ole fool.

"And don't worry. I know how to work a boat."

"You don't have to do this!" Skipper screamed, twisting his face away from his trappings, trying to find fresh air. He sucked metallic, blood-tinged breaths into his lungs, and bile rose in his throat. The pirate worked fast, wrapping them up like a burrito, with the ends folded over the top.

The distinctive screech of duct tape being torn from its roll penetrated Skipper's tomb only seconds before he felt it being secured to the tarp around him.

Dread crawled up his skin while sweat trickled down his face and neck. As the tape grew tighter, the air turned hot and thick, making him thrash against his fate.

"As soon as he fucked up, this was the only way today was going to play out." The pirate's hands worked fast and sure with the duct tape, securing the two men in the blue shroud.

Skipper knew he was going to be buried alive at sea. The one place that had always provided him solace.

Forever one with the vast expanse.

"No! You don't have to do this. I can help you fix what-ever he fucked up. I promise!" He tried thrashing against the tarp, but his tomb was secured. Maybe his fate had been sealed hours ago, and he was just catching on. "Please, don't do this." He whimpered as his hands worked feverishly to break free.

The man grunted, and Skipper froze, trying to make out every muted sound. As if listening would help him stop what was coming.

"For the love of God, man! At least kill me first. Knock me out. Don't do it this way. I never wronged you." Flailing with his feet, he couldn't kick free of the blood-drenched tarp.

Skipper's mind raced as his sarcophagus was dragged closer to the boat's edge. The pirate seemed to possess the strength of two men.

When the gate squeaked open, Skipper's bladder released. He tried talking faster, as if he could race to get out the right set of words to chart a new course.

It was too late to beg for his life. He understood that all too well. All he could hope for now was a quick death. "Just bash my head in. The gaff is right there! You can—"

The deck disappeared beneath him, and he began to fall.

Splash!

Another hit of adrenaline surged through Skipper as warm saltwater seeped through the folded edges of the plastic sheath, giving him the power to thrash even harder. Nothing gave. The tiny amount of slack he'd managed to make wasn't enough to get him out of this.

The bloody plastic pressed into his face, covering his mouth and nose as he panted in panic. The pressure of the ocean squeezed him tighter. A terrible ringing started in his ears, followed by a burst of dizzying pain.

Conserve your breath.

Water seeped onto his face, and he squeezed his eyes tighter. He knew he should blow out all his air. Empty his lungs and breathe in the saltwater for a quick end. It would be over faster if he stopped fighting the inevitable. But he just couldn't do it. The animalistic part of his brain overrode everything and made him keep fighting to stay alive.

Maybe the duct tape will hold long enough until I can work one hand free. There's still some air—

As if all of Skipper's sins came to bear, the duct tape tore away from one corner, and seawater rushed into his tomb. It filled his mouth, his ears, his eyes.

And as his lungs burned, desperate for air, Skipper's hope disappeared with the light as darkness enveloped him.

unfortunate but common high humidity of summer had blanketed the island. Heat baked and boiled everything that had washed up on the shore. Navigating around the displaced driftwood and broken pieces of homes and boats was bad enough. But now, rotting fish, seaweed, and jellyfish permeated the air with the pungent sting of death. And of course, there were two semisolid corpses decaying on the sand.

This was going to be a nightmare of a crime scene.

Senior Deputy Hoyt Frost had set up a perimeter around a slimy-looking lump of clothes, flotsam, and jetsam. She hoped that small pile wasn't supposed to be the two adult men she'd gotten the call about.

Her deputy was outside the taped-off area, talking with a man who was shifting from foot to foot while keeping his gaze focused squarely on the deputy's face.

As Rebecca got out of the cruiser, Hoyt glanced over. She tipped her chin up, signaling him to come to join her. If that nervous man with Hoyt was their only witness, she didn't want to go over the grisly details in his presence.

The kindhearted staff at the Shadow Island Community Health Center had cleaned her whole outfit, right down to polishing her badge and shining her shoes. She didn't want to get puke from the witness all over her toes if she could help it. And he looked close to losing his eggs and bacon.

Hoyt nodded his understanding and said something to the man before strolling over. The witness turned his back on the scene and stared at the ocean, taking breaths deep enough that Rebecca could see his shoulders move up and down.

They met at the edge of the crime scene. "What's up, Boss?"

After hauling sandbags and wrestling with a ladder in hurricane-force winds, Hoyt had been babying his recent surgery scar. She was worried he'd overdone things after just getting released to full duty.

"Darian can take over for you." She kept her voice low so no one else could hear them. "I'd like you to go see your doctor to make sure you didn't pull anything yesterday."

"No can do. Darian doesn't do beach scenes. And he's got other things to deal with." Hoyt shook his head but wouldn't meet her eyes.

Clearly, he was hiding something, but he didn't seem to be in any pain or move with difficulty. Even after driving stakes into the sand for the current crime scene, which he had to have done, he was standing up straight, so it couldn't be his physical health. She'd been keeping an eye on his condition since he'd come back from medical leave, so this had to be about Darian.

"How can he not do beach scenes? We're a beach town."

"Plenty of places in town that aren't sandy. One of us covers for him. Never been a problem before, isn't a problem now."

"But—"

Hoyt held up a hand. "Besides, I already called my doc and got cleared to work. He didn't even need to see me. He said I'm fine, and it's expected after what we went through. Said to just lay off the heavy lifting for a bit and treat it like a sore muscle, because that's all it is."

She frowned, wondering whether to believe him. "You sure?"

Instead of answering, he gestured at her bandaged hands. "Thankfully, you're here and can take over the heavy stuff. That is, if *you've* been cleared by your doc."

She realized he was trying to move the discussion away from Darian's reluctance to work a beach scene. She sighed, knowing he had to have a good reason. And Darian would too. He wasn't one to shirk his duties.

"Did that a few hours ago." The wounds on her hands itched like crazy but no longer hurt much. She'd gotten them during a successful rescue operation, so every ounce of pain had been worth it. "The bandages are just to keep debris out of the wounds so they can heal faster."

Hoyt seemed dubious but didn't argue. "If you say so."

"I do." She nodded toward the bodies, ready to get to the subject at hand. "Catch me up with what we've got here."

Hoyt rolled his shoulder and headed back in the direction of the witness, who was now diligently inspecting the stack of fishing gear piled at his feet. Rebecca walked alongside him.

"Two bodies washed ashore with the storm surge from Boris. They're higher than where high tide would have left them. That distinctive ridge from the tide was pretty much wiped out with the hurricane, so you'll need to just trust me on this."

Rebecca examined the area he indicated. "Any idea how long they've been here?"

"If they came with the surge, well, let's see." Hoyt scrunched his brow as he performed mental calculations. "I think it's safe to say they coulda been out here for twenty-four hours. There's not much left of their clothes, but the remaining scraps are fairly baked on. About the only good news is that they're far enough away from the incoming high tide that they won't be touched by the waves. I'd call this a body dump."

Rebecca snorted. "Dumped by the ocean instead of by a human. That's a first for me."

Hoyt chuckled softly, but then turned somber as they reached their witness. He made the introductions and jumped right into his questions. "Matt, can you tell the sheriff what you told me?"

Matt Brewster looked up from under the brim of his

straw hat and nodded, fiddling with the reel on his pole. There was nothing suspicious about his movements, just the nervous reaction of a man who'd seen something he wished he hadn't. A something that would haunt him the rest of his life.

"I came out to get some fishing in. After storms is the best time to catch the big fish. Then I saw that pile over there and," he swallowed thickly, "came over to see if it was storm debris, maybe someone's patio umbrella or something. Instead…poor bastards."

"What happened next?" Rebecca prompted.

"I called 911 as soon as I realized what it was. I also made sure I didn't get close to it. Didn't want to either. You can see where my tracks end. My tracks were the only ones on the beach when I got here too. I checked."

He pointed without looking, and Rebecca glanced over her shoulder. Just as Matt Brewster had said, one set of tracks stopped at least ten yards from the bodies. Another set was closer and circled the victims. Those were clearly Hoyt's as he left the beach, returned, and set up the crime scene tape.

"Second set of tracks is mine." Hoyt pulled the camera out of his pocket. "Made sure I took plenty of pictures before I got that close."

Rebecca didn't need her senior deputy's reassurances. She'd seen him at enough crime scenes to know he did his job correctly each time.

She glanced at the notepad Hoyt had used to jot down the initial information. It contained Matt Brewster's contact information, as well as his answers to the preliminary questions the deputy had asked. He'd covered everything.

She'd seen enough of the bodies from this distance to know there was no reason to ask if he recognized them. There weren't any faces left. And most likely, there weren't any brains either. Even from her current position, she'd seen the inside of at least one of the skulls. A few bits of skin remained, and she hoped the medical examiner would be able to get DNA for identifying the bodies.

"Thank you, sir. Since Deputy Frost has your contact information, you can go ahead and leave."

Brewster tipped his head. "I think I'll see how the fish are biting on the western side. I don't want to catch anything that might have bits of them in their bellies." As soon as the words were out of his mouth, he turned green. Nearly the same shade as the bloated corpses.

"Or maybe *not* try to catch any fish today. Just in case," Rebecca suggested.

Hoyt patted Brewster on the shoulder. "Maybe you should take a few minutes before you try anything."

Brewster nodded, gathered up his gear, and made his wobbly way down the beach away from the scene and the sickening smell.

Rebecca turned toward the mess that had once been humans. "Have you called forensics?"

Hoyt nodded. "Forensics and the M.E. are on their way. They should be here shortly. All the main roads are cleared, and the bridge didn't sustain any damage. We got lucky."

They sure had. Boris could have been much, much worse.

Rebecca glanced around the area and put her hands on her hips. "I don't suppose we have any more excuses to put off inspecting the bodies."

"Just make sure not to touch them." He gave her a haunted look and kicked his boots in the sand. "Bodies like these tend to pop."

"Yeah, and that possibility only gets more likely the longer they stay out here warming up." She looked up at the sun, which was still climbing in the sky. "Let's grab some mentholated ointment from my bag to slather under our noses. Once our sense of smell is masked, we can operate more efficiently."

The last time that trick had been used was so a group of technicians could process the vehicle of a suspect who had heartlessly trapped a puppy in the trunk on a hot day. Even with the salve, some of the techs had lost their lunch. Thank God, the puppy had pulled through.

After retrieving and applying the balm, Rebecca reached into the pouch on the back of her belt and pulled out her latex gloves. She put them on to cover her bandages, then pulled on a second pair to cover those.

The circling seagulls indicated she'd been right about the stench hanging thick in the air. She kept an eye on the birds as she ducked under the crime scene tape. The corpses would attract all kinds of scavengers, and she didn't want to get into a fight over rotting body parts.

The visible skins on the victims were blotchy and turgid, showing splits in several places as the flesh had soaked up more water than it could hold before being deposited on the land. Both corpses were utterly disfigured. And not just the skin. The muscles were sloughing off the bones. Some joints had already come apart in the arms, held somewhat together by scraps of clothing.

One of the vics' jaw was completely missing. Either from the turbulent current or predation, as fish moved into the mouth to eat out the tongue and throat before heading up into the skull. Soft tissues and small muscles tended to be devoured first because they were easy for the smaller sea life to consume before the bigger predators arrived to eat the large sections of meat.

There was no way they would be able to get any identification on the one without a jaw or teeth except through DNA.

"Crabs have already gotten to them. I've had to chase a

few off since I've been here. Ah, dammit. Get out of there, you nasty bastards." Hoyt swept his foot at two crabs munching on one of the legs. "This is why I never eat crab."

"Some Navy guys are the same way. One I knew said he never could be sure one of his fallen comrades wasn't in their bellies." Rebecca squatted down to get a better view and batted away another crab.

Both corpses appeared to be male. One was missing all the fingers from both hands. The torsos were split open and showed additional scavenging on their internal organs. Some organ tissues remained, in varying amounts, along with scraps of muscles and tendons.

She turned to face the ocean, wondering how big the fish in this area got. Some of the bites had nicked bone.

Combined with the terror and destruction of the hurricane the day before, the ocean didn't seem as warm and inviting as it had when Rebecca had first arrived on Shadow Island in the middle of the month.

Has it only been a few weeks? Wow.

Hoyt pushed his hat back on his forehead to wipe away sweat. "There's no way to tell where these two came from without phoning NOAA to ask them for tracking information after Boris blew through here. There're just too many factors we don't know to even hazard a guess as to how long they've been dead."

"What's the current pattern normally around here?" Rebecca made a mental note to study the sea surrounding her new home.

"The current comes from the north, but this stretch of the ocean is also known as the Graveyard of the Atlantic. Because of the piles of wrecked ships just below the surface."

Rebecca nodded. "I remember hearing that when I was a kid. Why does that happen?"

"Because the Labrador Current and the Gulf Stream meet

right around this area, but…" Hoyt shook a finger, "you can't count on that in this case. Boris came from the southeast and could have pulled them up with everything else. There's just no telling."

Rebecca nodded, leaned forward, and carefully lifted a piece of tattered clothing that might have been a flannel shirt. Salt-faded orange underneath caught her eye.

"Someone bound them with rope. There's blue plastic stuck to it as well."

Hoyt shook his head. "So I guess this *was* a body dump, not just poor unfortunates lost at sea."

She stood to examine the wrecked beach around them. "Twenty-four hours ago, we were shoveling sand into bags trying to hold back the rising water. Then we dropped everything to find out who turned a corpse into the embodiment of a mermaid."

Hoyt yanked off his gloves and stepped away from the scene. "And about died in the process."

Rebecca glanced at the corpses resting high on the shore. "Just when I thought Boris had stopped assaulting the island, he leaves us with these two. I can't believe I'm saying this, but this case might just be messier than the last one."

3

A second forensic van pulled up and parked beside Rebecca's white-and-tan cruiser. She waved at them but didn't move away from where she was waiting. Bailey had bagged the victims to keep the scavengers at bay and moved them into her van, but she was still on the beach, searching for missing parts.

The beach was now set up like an archeological dig, and Rebecca didn't want to get in the way of the professionals. When the fine-tined pitchforks had come out, she'd stepped away to protect the perimeter, knowing her role in this matter. She and Hoyt were just there to keep the lookie-loos away while the bodies were assembled and hauled off. Pieces she had thought were plant matter or maybe beached jellyfish had been scooped up and bagged as well—not as evidence, but as parts of the victims.

While Bailey had named each part based on their proximity to the bodies, Rebecca couldn't make heads or tails of where they'd fit into a human. It was past noon now, and it would take scientists to tell her if there was anything useful in what the M.E. had found.

"Just got word from my friend at the community health center." Viviane's voice crackled through Rebecca's radio. With nothing else to do, she and Rebecca had been chatting about the cleanup efforts that were going on throughout town.

"Good news, I'm hoping?"

So far, the aftermath had all been as positive as she could hope for after a strong Category 2 hurricane had swept over their little island. No buildings had been destroyed, the roads had all held up, and most miraculously, the bridge that connected them to the mainland had come through unscathed, if a bit cluttered with debris.

"No deaths, no serious injuries. At least, none related to the storm."

"Just the murder victim," Hoyt added, using his radio from the far side of the crime scene where he remained on guard.

"And the murderer too. He was stabbed. Can't forget him." Rebecca tried to take a sip of her coffee but found her cup empty. She moved to her trunk to pull out one of the water bottles she kept in every cruiser.

"Yup, just those." Rebecca was impressed at how Viviane rarely let dark reality dampen her good spirits. "The governor's office is already talking with Mayor Doughtie to see what we need to get everything back up and running. FEMA's managed to get some wheels turning, at least."

"All thanks to our fearless leader."

Rebecca rolled her eyes at Hoyt, who saw the gesture and laughed.

Before she could refute his claim, Viviane responded, "That's what everyone else is saying too."

"Guys," Rebecca sighed, "we all know Greg was the one who called the shots on the evacuation, and Hoyt was the one who—"

"Bah, that's the little stuff. I'm not saying we didn't do our jobs and do them well." Hoyt puffed up, and she smiled at his posturing. "We all did, which includes you. So take your due, Boss."

Compliments at work had never sat easily with Rebecca, so she chose to ignore them instead.

One of Bailey's assistants hopped out of the van and started walking toward her, holding several bags.

She took that excuse and ran with it. "Looks like we've got something new to look at, Frost."

"Is it soupy?" He peered over at the assistant to see what they had. "'Cause if it's soupy, I don't want to deal with it. You can keep that to yourself. And knowing Bailey and the tricks she likes to play, that's a real possibility." He continued to talk as Rebecca signed for the evidence and flipped the bag over to see what it was.

The label on the bag read *John Doe Two, personal possession.* "Not soupy. Just…slimy. It's a wallet."

"Oh, well, that's useful." Hoyt spat on the sand. "I'm betting it's not leather. Otherwise, that would have been eaten too."

Viviane made a retching sound. "See, that's why I don't eat seafood. You just don't know what those little critters have consumed."

Rebecca smiled and worked the bag around, maneuvering the open wallet to view the driver's license through its plastic sleeve. "Got a license here."

"Can you read it?"

"Barely. There's some bubbling of the plastic, and this thing is stuck in here pretty good. Probably from the moisture. I can't work it loose through the evidence bag." Rebecca peered harder. "I think the name is Samuel Graves, but I can't read the address. Does that name sound familiar to either of you?"

"Nope."

"Never heard of him. But maybe the M.E. has. She's headed your way, Boss."

Rebecca continued to manipulate the bag and saw at least two credit cards that had the same name on them. They were much easier to read. She only looked up when Bailey's feet appeared in her line of vision.

"Thought that might be helpful." Dr. Bailey Flynn wiped sweat off her forehead. "Is Frost not here?"

"He's on the other side of the cruiser, keeping the rubberneckers at bay. Do you have anything else for me?"

"Just some initial findings. You were right. The bodies were bound with rope. That's what took us so long. We had to get them separated and in their own bags without ripping them apart even more."

Rebecca pressed her hand to her belly. "That's terrible."

Bailey rotated her neck, working out the kinks. "One more thing. I noticed John Doe One has auburn hair while John Doe Two has dark hair. Two also had the remnants of an anchor tattoo on his neck, right side. There aren't any words on the bits that are left, but there's enough there to say it was an anchor. If there was more to it than just an anchor, I couldn't tell you."

Rebecca looked again at the driver's license photo inside the evidence bag. Without removing it from the protective bag and taking the license from the bubbled plastic wallet sleeve, she simply couldn't tell.

She shifted her line of thinking. "How long do you think they were out there?"

"That's where it gets harder. I found pieces of what appears to be tarp mixed in. So they were wrapped first, had time to decompose, then something compromised the bag, and the bigger predators were able to get in. That's why the soft organs are pretty much goners, but there are still some big meaty bits left."

Rebecca shook her head. "These poor men."

Bailey nodded. "At least they were dead when that happened."

That's something at least. "True."

"Anyway, the bigger scavengers couldn't get to them 'til recently. Fish will skeletonize a body in days out in the open ocean. Best I can tell you now is that the bodies have only been out of their tarp for a few days."

"Boris is the gift that keeps on giving. Thanks to him, we can't get a good timeline for these corpses." Rebecca shrugged. "On the flip side, we might never have found them without Boris, so there's that."

Bailey took off her gloves and pulled a bottle of water from a pocket in her jumpsuit. "Don't tell Frost, but I had to get some air. The smell doesn't bother me as much anymore, but all those gases in such a small area really suck the air out of it. We're going to be running the fans at full speed back in the morgue. After we get all the critters out of them."

Rebecca wrinkled her nose. "Out of them?"

Bailey took a long drink. "Oh yeah. There are plenty. We've been putting them into small containers, so they can also be analyzed back in the lab. Little buggers are all over. Found bigger bites too. Wherever they were dropped, it was deep ocean, not anywhere close by. Could even be some shark bites mixed in, but I'll have to get them under the lights to make sure of that."

"I've got a name at least. Samuel Graves."

"Never heard of him." Bailey bent over and pulled the booties from her shoes, tucking in her gloves before rolling them into a small, inside-out bundle. "I'm going to do one last check along the beach for the fingers and any other body parts, then we'll head off. As you know, I've got a full plate."

Rebecca snorted. "A full plate? I bet that's what the crabs thought too."

Bailey cocked her head to the side and smiled. "I knew I liked you. Your sense of humor is as dark as mine."

"I think you're just trying to butter me up, so I'll send Frost down later to get the updates."

At that, the M.E. burst out laughing. "If you do send him down, make sure he's wearing proper footwear this time."

Rebecca noticed Hoyt crane his neck, trying to see what they were laughing about on their side of the scene. She waved at him with a cheery smile. He turned away quickly.

"I had hoped to perform a virtual autopsy to determine if the COD was drowning or something else. Unfortunately, neither of our bodies have enough of the soft tissue remaining to use that method." Bailey finished untucking her pants from her socks and shook them out.

"Virtual?"

"Yeah, it's an MDCT. Think of it as a super CT scan. I haven't had a chance to use the process in a while and it looks like that streak will continue. It's probably just as well, since it would have been a bit time consuming to get the corpses in their current state of decomp into the machine."

Rebecca didn't look forward to helping move this human goo, but she'd volunteer if needed. "I can help if you need me to."

"Appreciate it. This is always a busy week for my office with the upcoming holiday. It's amazing how many people manage to kill themselves while celebrating their freedom. I'll let you know when I've found something."

The idea of deaths caused by drunken fireworks mishaps was not a pleasant one. "Okay, let me know when you've got anything new, and I'll let you know if I get any more information."

A car pulled into the parking lot, and Rebecca broke away to deal with it.

The make, model, and spotless appearance of the vehicle should have clued her into the drama that was about to erupt as the driver's door flung open.

Richmond Vale, chairman of the Select Board and a royal pain in Rebecca's ass, was already glaring at her as he slammed his door shut. He stormed over, scowling at the forensic techs working through the sand and bagging items. "What's going on here, now?"

And hello to you, too, you pompous asshole.

Knowing her face would betray her thoughts, Rebecca turned to inspect the area as well. "Crime scene cleanup right now."

"How can you have something like this on our beaches? Our beaches! We need these beaches pristine and inviting. Tourist season is well under way, and this is always one of our biggest weekends. How are we supposed to get visitors here if you've got crime scene tape up all over the place?"

Is he serious?

"Well, if I hadn't put the tape up, our visitors would have gotten the gelatinous remains of other tourists on their shoes. I would think that would be even worse for tourism."

His eyes popped wide. "Remains? Are you telling me we've had another murder? That's—"

"No idea if it's a murder." She didn't want to hear about how many deaths there had been in the last few weeks. "They're just bodies that washed ashore with the hurricane. ID on one corpse indicates he wasn't local. They may not even be from our state."

That seemed to calm Vale down a little.

"They're not locals? Or tourists?"

"We have no open missing persons cases, so I doubt it. Neither one has been positively ID'd, though."

He waved a hand toward the crime scene. "Well, get this off the beach right away. We need to show people we're a good place to take the family to relax."

Rebecca dipped her hands in her pockets, so she wouldn't slap the man.

"That section will be pristine long before you get those trees cut up and hauled off." She pointed to the north where three trees were wedged into the sand.

Vale's eyes narrowed. "Don't tell me how to do my job. You just make sure yours is done right and you don't chase off the money that keeps this town running."

With a low growl, he turned and stomped back to his car, already pulling his phone out of his pocket to yell at someone else.

Rebecca glared at his back as he went off to deal with more important matters.

"Welcome to Shadow Island, where human lives are worth less than a clean beach."

S amuel Graves had a missing persons report opened on him already. Rebecca sat in her patrol cruiser, trying to stay out of the early afternoon sun to read up on him. His license indicated he did live in Virginia after all, and the missing persons report had been filed just last week.

There was a picture to go along with that report, but the smiling man looked nothing like the unfortunate one discovered on the shore. On closer examination, the image showed an ornate anchor tattoo on his neck, right where Bailey said she'd found traces of one. All signs pointed to Samuel Graves being John Doe Two.

Hopefully, there was a next of kin who could match DNA. That would be the only way they could confirm this was indeed the missing man.

Except she had two bodies. Would she be lucky enough to find a second missing persons report that matched her spare corpse? As she pulled up information from the missing persons case, movement outside her window made her look up.

Ryker Sawyer smiled as he walked through the parking lot, heading right for her.

Suddenly nervous and excited, she brushed her hair back, and closed the laptop. A quick glance around the beach showed that everything was still under control. Forensics was still doing their job and not paying any attention to her. Hoyt had been keeping his distance ever since he heard Bailey laugh, so she didn't have to worry about him catching her flirting on the job.

She rolled down the window. "Hey, you, what are you doing out here?"

His dimples deepened. "I was in the area for work, saw you sitting here, and wondered if you've had lunch yet."

Rebecca checked the time and saw it was just after one. She'd been ignoring her growling stomach for more than an hour. "No, I haven't. And it doesn't look like I'll get it anytime soon either."

"That's too bad. I wanted to take you, my treat, if you were about to wrap things up." He glanced over at the scene and shrugged. "But I can see now's a bad time. I was afraid that would be the reality of it, so I brought this just in case." He held out the travel mug he'd brought with him.

"What's this?" She took the cup and tilted it to look inside.

"Coffee. You take it with lots of cream and one sugar, right?" His smile was hopeful and widened as she nodded.

She was just as touched by his knowing how she took her coffee as she was that he'd thought to bring her something. "I do. Thanks." She started to take a sip, but he placed his hand on the top of the mug, and her lips brushed the back of his hand.

His nostrils flared at the sensation. "But there's a catch."

She raised an eyebrow, and he laughed and pulled his hand back.

"You have to return the cup."

That worked perfectly for her, so she decided to up the ante. "Over dinner?"

Ryker brightened. "Are you asking me out, Rebecca West?"

"I am, Ryker Sawyer. Open-ended, though, since we both have a lot of work going on right now."

He grew somber as he twisted back and forth, looking at the disaster area they were standing in the middle of. "We're both good at our jobs, so I'm sure we can figure something out."

"Speaking of work. What are you doing at the beach?"

"I was hired to help clean up the debris. But with you guys out here, I'll probably head over to the boardwalk and see what needs patching there, instead. Vale called and reamed me about the trees over here, but like hell I'm going to run a chainsaw so close to a crime scene."

Rebecca bit her lip as her cheeks heated with guilt. "Uhm, that might be my fault. He came down here to yell at me for having a crime scene on his tourist beach, and I told him that we'd be cleaned up before those trees were. I didn't mean to sic the psycho on you."

As bad as she felt for what she'd done, Ryker just laughed. "Honestly, that guy is such a nuisance, I've actually considered dropping the contract because of him. It's not big and probably isn't worth it to put up with his crap. I did it for the possibility of scoring future contracts, but some people are going to shit-talk no matter how well you do your job. And that's no good for us contractors."

"Life's too damn short to put up with people like him."

He gestured to the forensic van. "I bet that's something you learned on the job."

And in life.

"Learned when I lost my parents, actually." As Ryker's

expression morphed into guilt, she grimaced at her thought-less words. "I didn't mean it like that. Just that I enjoyed every minute I had with them and that's what got me through the bad times following their deaths. When you're with someone you love, the little men like Vale don't matter at all. So I don't waste any time on them."

He studied her face intently as she spoke, nodding. "I like that. He's like a rock in your shoe. They can be removed and forgotten, but the person you're walking with won't ever be."

"Exactly." She smiled. He'd taken her clumsy attempt at philosophy and reworded it so simply that it made even more sense to her now.

"Then if you'll excuse me, I'm going to go get rid of this rock from my shoe so I can be ready for the good things to come." He winked. "Call me when you get a chance to eat today."

She wanted to reach for him, to tell him to come back. Instead, she waved. "If it's not too late."

She watched him walk toward the boardwalk. It was chock-full of people who were too timid, or smart, to come down to the beach to see what was going on.

"I hope you're seeing this, Vale. No one was chased off." Rebecca watched a father lift his son onto his shoulders so the child could get a better view. And then he snapped a picture of the crime scene. "This might be better business for you than a pristine beach."

5

Though there were more people here than I'd expected, the boardwalk wasn't too crowded. From the conversations overheard on my walk, I could tell most of them were locals—waving familiar hellos to me—but there were still some who had driven down. What they thought a tiny tourist town like this could offer so soon after a hurricane hit, I had no idea.

I wasn't there to gawk at the destruction, though. Or to fish. Neither of those interested me. It was what I'd heard on the noon news that convinced me to meander through the lookie-loos. A report about two bodies, bound together, that had washed up on the shore.

Hiding in plain sight among the throng of people on the boardwalk was easy enough. Plenty of them were watching the police activity below as well, so I blended in as usual. Just so my interest didn't stand out too much, I made sure to move to a different spot every hour or so. Put on a jacket or took it off. Swapped out different caps too. In case the cops were videoing the crowd, I wouldn't stand out too much. They were always easy to fool with such simple tactics.

I hadn't thought it could be my guys washed up on the shore that morning, but I'd heard enough from the other rubberneckers to realize that the details seemed to align with what I'd done. Once I knew that, there was no way I could stay away. It took some subtlety, but I managed to chat up enough people to find someone with photos they'd snapped of the bodies when they were still beached on the sand. Like bloated, sunbaked whales.

Oh, how I wish I'd seen them that way. By the time I'd made my way to the scene, the bodies had been bagged and shielded from curious onlookers. The photos taken by the macabre Good Samaritan would have to do. And honestly, the blobs in the images bore little resemblance to the men I'd tossed overboard a few weeks ago. Just like I had warned them, they'd fed the fish. And the fish had eaten well.

There was still some skin left, sure.

The damn hurricane was a stroke of bad luck. I'd begun to think I was in the clear, but now here I was, watching the cops go through the evidence. One upside of the storm was that there was so much washed up on that beach that there'd be no way to link the murders to me. As expected, they were picking up everything, and almost none of it had anything to do with my stunt.

While the crowd had their eyes on the activity in the sand, my attention drifted to the cops.

There was a woman on the force, and oddly, the techs and deputy seemed to treat her like a boss. I liked the old sheriff —liked how he turned a blind eye to most things. Would having a new sheriff complicate things? Luck had never been on my side, which was why I always had to think two steps ahead.

Maybe it was time to call my buddy in the Yacht Club and see if he could help. If that woman was officially in charge now, I needed to know. Surely, they'd handpicked her or gotten her on their side somehow.

They always made sure of that.

That would be tricky, though. None of this was a Yacht Club matter. It was purely personal.

But the bodies were way more intact than I thought they'd be. Maybe they weren't mine after all. It was a big ocean and there was no way I was the only one dropping bodies. Yeah, that had to be it. Hell, maybe these *were* Yacht Club-related.

I'd keep an eye on things just in case, but even if they were the pair I'd dropped, there was nothing to tie them to me. I'd made a clean break. But if anyone managed to link them to me, well, there were plenty of hungry fish left in the ocean.

Rebecca had only been back in the office for an hour. It was past dinnertime when they finished at the beach, so she'd stopped to pick up takeout. After having only a small breakfast and then missing lunch, she'd been starving and still had work to get done before she could head home. Thankfully, there wasn't much paperwork to deal with. Not yet, at least.

No positive identification, no primary crime scene, no witnesses, no cause of death, and barely any human remains. There really wasn't much for her to work with right now. The folder she'd put together for this case was dismally empty. High-resolution images of bodies whose lines had been blurred by decay wouldn't help her much.

Tomorrow, once all the evidence logs were sent over, there would be plenty to do. Earlier, she'd left a message for the detective in charge of the missing persons case on Samuel Graves. Right now, the only thing she had to work with were the pictures they'd taken of the scene. She flipped between three images of the head of the fingerless victim, John Doe One, all taken at different angles. Something about the skull looked off to her, and she made a note to ask Bailey if he'd been struck in the head.

Rebecca popped the last bite of her burrito into her mouth and wiped her fingers on a napkin so she could type with both hands again. Once she wrote up an affidavit to get a warrant to pull banking and credit card records, she could head home and finally relax. Those records should have been pulled for the missing persons case, but she didn't see them listed anywhere.

A knock on the doorframe made her look up as she continued to type. Hoyt was standing there, shaking his head. Dread had settled in by the grim look on his face, and she waited for him to say they had another dead body somewhere.

"Were you really eating while going through those pictures?"

She covered her lips with her fingertips to hide her smile as she worked on finishing chewing so she could swallow. "It's not like I was eating sashimi or anything."

Hoyt gagged dramatically and bent over holding his stomach. "Oh, that's not even funny."

Despite what he thought, she laughed, then had to grab her napkin to keep from spewing crumbs on her desk. "I'm laughing."

He finished overacting and stood up again. "Are you at least going to go home sometime soon?"

She finished wiping her mouth and leaned back in her chair. "Yeah, I need to finish this paperwork for the judge, then I'll be taking the cruiser home."

Hoyt leaned on the door and crossed his arms. "Isn't your truck in the parking lot? Do you think something will come up that you need the cruiser?"

"My baby's out there, yeah. But she's not running right, and I couldn't find the time to call a mechanic to look her over. With all the water I drove through yesterday, I don't want to make things worse by driving her home if she just needs to finish drying out."

"That's a good plan. But I've got a better one." Hoyt leaned out the door and called down the hallway. "Hey, Darian! Come here."

"What?" Darian's response was tagged by the sound of boots.

"Sheriff's truck is messing up after all the rain yesterday. I know you've got tools in your Jeep. Can you go take a look and see what's wrong?"

"I'm busy!" Despite the refusal, Darian's footsteps hadn't halted.

"No, you're not!" Hoyt yelled back. "You've been sitting at your desk and looking at pictures of your baby girl for the last hour. West has something else to deal with."

Darian appeared in her doorway. "Keys?"

With a grateful smile, Rebecca tossed him her keys.

"Wish me luck."

Rebecca crossed her fingers. "Good luck."

Hoyt pushed off the door. "See? It's good to be the boss. Nearly as good as being the senior deputy. I'm gonna head out now. My shift was over hours ago, and Angie's waiting. I still have a yard to clean up too."

"Good night, Frost. And thanks."

"Yeah, Boss." Hoyt waved over his shoulder as he walked out.

Alone again, Rebecca threw away her wrapper, finished her request for the warrant, then decided to check more into her possible victim. Calling his friends and family would be out of line, considering they hadn't confirmed it was Graves. It would be emotionally damaging for everyone if that was how they found out about his death. With so little to go on, she turned to the internet.

Pay dirt.

Surprising for a man his age, Graves had a sizeable social media presence that included a professional website with a fair number of favorable reviews for his business. Samuel "Skipper" Graves ran a boat charter business out of Norfolk, Virginia that did boat tours, fishing expeditions, and, in the winter months, whale-watching day cruises.

There were plenty of pictures for her to look through, a portal to schedule a reservation, and a link to his Better Business Bureau account for Coastal Tours, the name of his company. The man looked happy and lively in the pictures, most of which were taken on his boat or on the dock next to it. She clicked through them for a while, noting that he seemed to have a lot of friends, and he even came off as charming in his photos.

She found the history tab and read his bio, about why he'd started a new career more than twenty years ago. After retiring from working on a fishing boat, he'd bought his own and focused on the joys of sharing his love of boating with those who wanted the same thing. It was a passion project he'd turned into a paying career. He was a true American Dream story.

On the surface, at least.

She continued to dig into him, and thanks to all the handy links he had on his website, including a Facebook, Instagram, and LinkedIn profile, her job was made easier.

Graves had been renting the same building for the last thirteen years, and when she checked into that address, she saw another name listed. In fact, another business was registered at the same location. The second one was run by a man named Andy Woodson.

When Rebecca looked into him, she found a very similar website. Woodson rented out kayaks, canoes, and paddleboards. It was a nicely related business that she was sure worked well with Graves's charter service. Looking at a picture of Woodson, she recognized him from several of the photos she'd seen on Graves's website.

Rebecca added that name to her possible contacts list but saw that it was after closing time for both businesses, so she decided to wait until tomorrow to try calling. Hopefully, by then, she would have a definite answer on whether John Doe Two was Graves. It wouldn't be the first time in her career she'd found a body with someone else's wallet on it.

Besides, she hadn't been able to talk to the officer in charge of the original missing persons case yet, and she didn't want to step on any toes. Even if his toes didn't seem to be anywhere near the case currently.

Her search had taken her less than an hour, but she at least had a solid foundation of who Graves was, assuming he was, in fact, one of the bodies who'd been deposited on her beach. With nothing else to go on and nothing else to do, Rebecca turned off her computer and gathered her things.

She was closing her door when Darian called out to her. "You're all set."

"So it was a simple fix like I thought?"

"Yup. It was just a couple of wet spark plugs. I sprayed them down with WD-40 and they're running fine now. But you'll need to replace those worn covers. If you bring new covers into the station one day, I can do that for you." He tossed the keys back to her and she had to juggle her coffee cup in order to catch them, which made him laugh. "She runs fine now."

"Thanks, I appreciate it. I knew they needed replacing, but I haven't found the time since I got here." Rebecca tucked her keys into her pocket and gave a relieved sigh. "I owe you one."

"No problem. I wrapped some electrical tape around

them for now, just to seal them up." He studied her for a moment and seemed to be chewing something over.

She just knew he was going to ask her about it.

"So you do know what you need to do for engine maintenance?"

And there it was. "I know. I just…" Her cheeks heated up a bit. It was so embarrassing to know how to do something but not be able to do anything about it because of a stupid smell. It would have been even more embarrassing to try and fix the problem herself just to puke all over her engine in the parking lot.

She didn't even get to say anything before his face turned grim, but there was understanding in his eyes, and he waved her off.

"Is it a trigger?"

The casual way he talked about something so catastrophic caught Rebecca off guard. The skin around her eyes tightened, and she bit her lip, trying not to think about it. She tried not to remember the stink of used engine oil soaked into the cold concrete mixed with the smell of her own blood. She raked the keys over her thumb to distract her mind and worked to control her breathing. She could feel his eyes take in her every tiny movement.

"I got you. No worries. Had a buddy with the same problem after his convoy was ambushed. His was the smell of gasoline."

"Engine oil." Rebecca answered his unspoken question as she breathed out, then lifted her head and took a deep breath in through her mouth.

He just nodded, as if it didn't matter. And maybe to him, it didn't.

"I read about an FBI shoot-out in a parking garage in D.C. that ended with an unnamed agent sent to the hospital. I can put two and two together. Don't worry about it. We've got your back."

Rebecca blew out her breath. She wanted to rage about it. To rant about how stupid it was that she could have such a reaction to something so insignificant. But the look in his eyes made her realize he understood her problem all too well.

"Just don't give me any grief when I have to stop and get sand out of my boots. Okay?"

That made her freeze, and she was glad she hadn't said anything after all. Now the understanding look in his eyes made sense. He wasn't being empathetic because his boss had PTSD. He understood her because he, too, dealt with unresolved trauma. Somehow, that made it a lot better, and her right shoulder started to relax.

"Is that your trigger?"

Darian gave a one-armed shrug, again as if it didn't matter. But she knew it did. Just as much as hers did.

Sand. Who would have thought?

But that made sense too. Darian was ex-Army. More than likely, he'd done at least one tour in the Middle East. The ones who made it back called it the Sandbox for a reason.

Rebecca dropped her head and chuckled. "And you live in a beach town. That's rough, man."

"Oh, yeah, it is. My wife loves the beach."

"I'll never ask you to work a beach scene, then."

"And I'll take care of whatever maintenance you need on your truck." He started to turn away before stopping with a grimace. He pinched his lips, like he didn't want to say anything, but then spoke in a rush. "We kind of have a code for it. 'He has something else to deal with.' It's silly, but it works and keeps people from asking too many questions. And I *am* dealing with something, it'll just take me a few more years to do so."

"That's why when Hoyt said I had something else to deal with, you knew exactly what he was talking about."

"We take care of our own here, sir."

She felt shitty about it now, but she had to confess. "You know, I almost called you out to the scene today."

He grinned. "But you didn't. Because Hoyt's got both our backs. The man is like a second father to me. He's pure gold."

7

The main streets were busy with people when Hoyt Frost pulled into the employee parking lot at the sheriff's station to start work. It had only been a day, but already, most of the commercial streets were cleared of wayward hurricane debris. As always, blue tarps had bloomed on several houses after the heavy storms, but he knew those would start disappearing once people replaced missing shingles and patched any holes.

Ladders were leaning against several businesses, with workers swarming up and down them, hauling materials. He took a moment to stand there and appreciate the scene. His town never failed to fill him with pride as the citizens came together to help each other through rough times.

There was a tiny pang in his heart as he thought about how little he'd done to help his neighbors before. West's words about protecting himself and his family when it came to the Yacht Club still haunted him and filled him with shame and regret. Of course, the worst part was that she was right.

When Walter had been stranded on his roof, Hoyt hadn't

wasted a thought about helping him down. When the levees broke, he hadn't hesitated to head right for them, even though he knew he could be washed out to sea by the waves. That thought had been pestering him ever since he'd seen the bloated bodies on the beach. A fate like those two men received was exactly what he'd been risking while he worked through the hurricane.

But it hadn't slowed him down, or any of the rest of them. They'd all been out working the preparations, mostly without complaint. Yet, somehow, they'd all been cowed over the years to avoid the Yacht Club for fear of…what exactly?

Having a case tossed? Letting a bad guy get off on a technicality? Having to testify in court? Even getting shot was better than watching his neighbors suffer. Why had he let it go on for so long?

Because that's the way we always did it.

Hoyt stepped out of the shadow of the building and kept watching his neighbors fix this and clean up that. One man was struggling to lift a sheet of plywood up the ladder, and a woman passing by stopped and helped him adjust the strap he was using to haul it up. Once it was settled, they exchanged nods, and she continued on her way.

But it's not. This *is the way we always did things. Helping each other out. Watching out for each other. Working together to take on jobs that are too big for one person.*

Regret at all the things he hadn't done, the times he'd looked the other way, filled Hoyt, and he dropped his gaze to his boots.

Morning light glinted off the snaps of his belt. Lifting his gaze to his chest, he stared at the badge reflecting the rising sun. He had to do better. He *would* do better. No more looking away. No more allowing evil to hide in the shadows.

He would do better. For his neighbors. For his town. For his family.

He had to prove to himself that he was just as good of a person as they all were to him. And that was when a brilliant idea hit, and he knew exactly what he was going to do as soon as he got to his desk.

Viviane was already in, and he was confident she'd be more than happy to help put his plan into action. With renewed pride, he turned to go inside, then saw a grimy, disheveled man with a long, scraggly beard walking down the street.

The man stopped at the first bench he came to that was out of the bright sun and sat down. The old, flimsy plastic bag he was holding fell at his feet as he leaned back and closed his eyes. Exhaustion lined his sunburned face as he relaxed in the shade.

Checking both ways, Hoyt crossed the street and walked over. The man looked vaguely familiar, and his eyes snapped open as the deputy approached. Apprehension filled them before Hoyt could smile, finally recognizing him. This was the latest renter at the Seashell Hostel on the edge of town.

"Hey, Mac. We met a couple of weeks back. Officer Frost. How you doing?"

The ragged man sat forward and scooped up his bag. "Not good, Officer. I was just trying to rest for a bit, if that's okay?"

Hoyt shrugged and stepped up to the bench. "That's what public benches are for. To rest on. But you look beat, young man, like a bench isn't going to cut it."

Mac worked the bag into his fingers to keep it from tearing more.

"Maybe, but the hurricane destroyed my room. Lost most of my stuff too."

Hoyt grimaced at that, remembering that one of the fallen trees had landed on the hostel, smashing out all the windows. "I hope you weren't in there when that happened." He examined the man but didn't see any obvious signs of cuts or wounds.

"Naw, landlady evacuated us to the shelter before then. But now she won't let me in. The place is closed, and I don't have anywhere else to go. I had to sleep in the park last night with a few other guys."

"There's a FEMA tent set up at the school. You can sleep on the bunks there 'til the hostel opens back up."

Mac shrugged. "I got no car, either, so I'd have to walk. I've got a buddy that's going to help me out today."

"Well, if you need, head over to the church on Spring Street. The pastor there can hook you up with a good meal and some clothes. He can probably get you a ride if you need it."

The man brightened at that. "Thanks. I'll head over as soon as I get a nap."

"Have a good day. If you need any help, let me know." When Mac nodded but didn't say anything more, Hoyt turned and left him to it. All he could do was offer the man help. He couldn't make him accept it.

With a wave, he crossed the street again and headed to work.

"Good morning." Viviane grinned as she let him through to the back.

"Morning. How are you doing this fine day?" Hoyt headed for the coffeepot to top off his cup. He looked around the station but didn't see anyone else.

Viviane, who had turned to watch him as he walked through, grimaced and rolled her eyes when she saw him looking. "He's not here. Wasn't here when I got here either."

Trent Locke was the "he" in question.

Hoyt let out a disgruntled sigh and plopped down at his desk. "His cruiser's here."

Viviane shrugged. "Melody said he left just after five and didn't come back. She didn't check on the cruisers, though."

"She shouldn't have to. Locke knows when he's scheduled. None of us should have to keep tabs on him. Let's see if he at least filled out his log."

Annoyed at the junior deputy's continuous slacking off, Hoyt signed into his computer, putting serious thought into no longer covering for the man. As a department, they needed to start doing better now that they were taking on harder cases. Locke was the weak link in their chain. He needed to toughen up or get tossed.

Sadly, Hoyt knew which of the choices it would probably be.

8

R ebecca felt refreshed and lighthearted as she walked through the station door. She took a sip from her travel mug and smiled again. It was the same cup Ryker had given her the day before, and she hoped to return it to him today.

All she had to do was wrap up a double homicide, wherein at least one victim lived and worked more than forty-five minutes away. And manage the fact that the crime may have occurred in international waters. And ID the other vic. And find who was responsible for their deaths.

She wrinkled her nose as she stepped onto the carpet. Gross. It was no longer damp, but she made a mental note to get the nasty thing replaced.

Yup, just take care of a few minor things, and she'd be free to have dinner with Ryker tonight. Rebecca snorted as she peered over her mug toward dispatch.

"Morning, Viviane. How was your night?"

Viviane smiled and did a little shimmy in her chair. "Oh, it was good. We should get drinks soon, and I'll tell you all about it."

Rebecca raised her eyebrows, and Viviane responded with a coy smile. "Maybe things will slow down enough for us to do that."

"Oh, don't say it like that!" Viviane waved her hands at Rebecca as if she were shooing something away. "You'll jinx us. And I need some girl time to unwind and gossip before the bars get filled up with more out-of-towners."

"No jinxing." Rebecca laughed and crossed her fingers. "I could use some girl time too. My news may not be as hot as yours, but it's keeping me warm right now." She took a sip of her coffee as she let herself into the bullpen.

"I noticed the new travel mug. Is there a story behind it?" Viviane propped her chin on her hand and waited for Rebecca to spill.

"A little one. But I did manage to use it to secure a date." She held up a hand before Viviane could interrupt with a string of questions. "At an undecided time and date in the future."

"You're saying we need to get this case handled first?" At Rebecca's nod, Viviane turned and pointed down the hall. "Then you'll be pleased to know you got a warrant faxed over this morning."

"Already off to a good start. Fingers crossed 'til dinnertime."

Hoyt looked up as Rebecca made her way in. "Speaking of *fingers*, our second John Doe, the one *with* fingers, is Samuel Graves. Bailey sent over confirmation this morning." He took a sip from his coffee while reading from his computer screen. "She had to put together the pieces of skin still present on his neck before photographing the remnants of the anchor tattoo. With some detail she found at the top and along one edge, she's confident the tattoo matches what's visible in his driver's license photo and missing persons report."

"That's all the ID we're going to get, I'm guessing." Rebecca imagined telling the wrong family their missing loved one had washed up on their island and winced.

"Right. Water, critters, and the air did a number on the body, so sadly, the decomposition destroyed any fingerprints he had. But Bailey's thorough. If she's confident, I'm confident." He passed over a sheet of paper printed with company info. "Anyway, Graves ran a charter service out of Norfolk called Coastal Tours. No ID on the digit-less John Doe."

Taking the paper, Rebecca stepped over to the coffee maker. "I looked him up last night, just in case the wallet was planted to throw us off his real identity. Graves had a man he shared a building with. They might even be business partners." She finished topping off her cup and turned around. "Why don't you come back to my office, and I can show you what else I discovered?"

Hoyt followed her to her office and waited until she sank into her super-comfy desk chair, complete with lumbar adjustment, before taking a seat himself.

"I left a message for the detective on the case in Norfolk. Hopefully, he's responded. I did loop him in about the bodies we found, but we'll have to update him on Bailey's positive ID." She checked her phone but didn't see the light indicating she had a voicemail. Viviane would have told her if she'd gotten a call through the station.

"And you got a warrant to go through his banking records?"

Rebecca lifted the faxed approval from the top of her desk and examined it. "That and the credit cards he had in his wallet. That way, we can see if there was any activity on them after he was last seen. I'm still waiting to get the full report from Norfolk."

"Want me to dig into that?"

"Yeah. While you're doing that, I'll see if I can reach the

man he shares a building with, Andy Woodson, and see what he can tell me."

"Sounds good. I'll get on it." Hoyt rose and headed back to his desk while she checked the file online. The detective hadn't responded yet. That was certainly annoying.

Putting that aside for now, Rebecca picked up the phone and called Coastal Tours.

"Coastal Tours. Sorry, but we're not operating boat tours right now."

"Andy Woodson?"

There was a slight pause. "Yes, ma'am, how can I help you?"

"Mr. Woodson, this is Sheriff West from Shadow Island. I'm looking into the missing persons case of Mr. Samuel Graves and would—"

"Oh, shit. He's dead, isn't he? Heard on the news about a couple bodies washing up down on Shadow Island. You wouldn't be calling from that island unless one of them was his."

She was surprised at how quickly Woodson put that together and felt immediate regret that she wasn't present to see his reaction when he learned of his business partner's death. "Yes, sir, I'm sorry. We identified a body we found."

"Shit. Shit." His sentiments were followed by heavy breaths that she thought were going to turn into sobs. "Shit."

"I'm very sorry for your loss, Mr. Woodson. Would you be willing to speak with me about Mr. Graves?"

"Yeah." There was another pause and the sound of several deep breaths. "Can you come here? I need to close up and… pull myself together. We shared this business, and now that I know he's not coming back, I need to handle some things."

"Yes, sir." That suited Rebecca just fine. She'd planned on telling him of Graves's death in person, but his instincts had her changing course.

"Ignore the closed signs when you get here. Just knock."

"It will take me a couple of hours."

"That's fine. It's going to take me that long to process all this."

As sad as Samuel Graves's death seemed to be for Andy Woodson, this was a plus for the case. Hopefully, his former partner could offer some valuable insights. The man clearly knew Graves reasonably well if he was this affected.

Or else, he's a good actor.

9

Rebecca pulled into the Backwater Marina just before noon. It was a basic storefront adorned with a mural of various water sports being enjoyed by picture-perfect families. As Woodson had warned, a closed sign was hanging on the window.

At the door, she unhooked her badge from her belt. A man with long gray hair pulled back in a ponytail stood at the register. She tapped on the glass. When he looked up, she flashed her badge. Once her credentials registered, he nodded, and walked over to unlock the door.

"Sheriff West?"

"Yes, sir. And you're Andy Woodson?" She stepped inside, and he locked the door behind her.

He wiped his cheek. "That's me. Call me Andy. I'm sorry. I'm not dealing with this very well. Skipper, that's what everyone called Samuel, he was..." Woodson sighed heavily and waved his hand at the walls. "I never thought he'd...not make it back. It's like hearing Superman died in mid-flight. I kept checking the slip to see if the boat ever came back, at least, but I haven't seen it since. I know the local cops and Coast Guard were checking, too, but I don't know what they found, if anything."

Rebecca's gaze followed where he had waved. The walls were filled with pictures. Most were Skipper on his boat, on the beach, on a boardwalk. He was holding up fish, standing next to a six-foot marlin, water skiing, pointing at a whale breaching water, smirking from behind the wheel of a boat, and, in a couple, he was sitting at a table holding up a beer. In all the pictures, he was smiling. There were other people in several of them too. Some of them matched the ones she'd seen online, but there were many more here.

"He seemed well-liked."

"Superman might be exaggerating a bit, but Skipper was like everyone's favorite uncle. Whether you'd just met him or known him for years. And now he's gone. When his boat didn't come back, I didn't think much of it at first." He went back to the register and picked up where he'd left off. "Figured he was having good luck with the fishing or something and didn't want it to end. But then he was gone for ten days. That wasn't like him. When he didn't answer on the radio or the satellite phone, I knew something was wrong and filed a report last week."

Rebecca gestured at the pictures. "None of his family noticed he was missing?"

Woodson shook his head but didn't meet her eyes. "His only living blood family is his brother, Eldridge. He has Alzheimer's and lives in a nursing home Skipper paid for. No idea what's going to happen to him now."

"No wife or girlfriend or boyfriend?" With how Woodson was acting, she wondered if they were more than business partners. His unwillingness to maintain eye contact indicated he was hiding something.

But he just shook his head and kept going through his paperwork. "No one I knew of. I can't say if he was gay or straight either. I never noticed anyone he was interested in. He kept those things to himself. I don't think he was gay, but I never saw him with a woman either." He shrugged. "Men our age aren't really open about things like that. That was his business and his alone."

"You said he was out on his boat. Do you know where he was going?"

"He didn't have anything booked for the twelfth, when he left, so wherever he was going was personal. That wasn't uncommon. He'd take his boat out on his own and just enjoy a few days or a week at sea."

Rebecca decided to test if Woodson knew more about Skipper's death than he was letting on. He'd not yet asked *how* his friend died. *Because he doesn't want to know, or because he already knows?*

"So it's possible he was drinking or doing other things while he was out that could have led to his death?"

She'd checked the news on her drive over, and nothing had been published that even hinted at the bodies being murder victims. In fact, most of the reports seemed to assume they were victims of rough seas from the hurricane, not human malice. Rebecca still had a lot to learn about the circumstances of the deaths, but she knew the two men were dead long before Boris ravaged Shadow Island. Knowing more about the facts of the case than the media would work to her advantage.

"Skipper wasn't like that. He liked his drink well enough, but he never got drunk while captaining the boat. Swore that's how he lived so long. It only takes one drunk at the helm to kill or seriously injure someone. He used to say that all the time. He kept most of his drinking for poker nights. No way was he going to risk his passengers or his business."

"You mentioned this was a personal trip. How do you know that?"

Woodson reached over and pulled up a ledger. "He didn't have anyone scheduled in his book."

"He kept a travel log?" Rebecca reached for it. After a slight hesitation, Woodson handed the ledger to her.

"It's not a travel log. That's where we log our rentals and reservations."

"Our?" She flipped the ledger open and scanned through the entries. It was set up like an old-fashioned hotel register, where the rentals and expected hours were written on the left with dates and times. In the right column, the customer would sign in and out. The dates were filled out with the last entry for yesterday.

"Well, yeah. I use it, too, for my rentals. My gear isn't as expensive as his boat, but I still need to keep track of it all." He scratched his cheek. "You wouldn't believe how many extra rentals we get from people seeing what else has been rented in the past. It's like they want to compete with everyone else."

"Do you mind if I take this with me?" Rebecca closed the ledger and held it down by her side, hoping she wouldn't need to request another warrant.

"Uhm, don't you need a warrant or something to take that?" Woodson shifted back and forth on his feet but still didn't meet her eyes.

"As you said, this is a shared ledger. If you give me permission, I can simply take it. If you need me to get a warrant, I can do that in a few hours." She waited patiently to see if he would argue. She wasn't bluffing. This ledger should have been in evidence already for the missing persons case, so either she could get it for her murder case, or the locals could.

"No, it's fine. I'll…it's not like I need to record any more rentals on it." He sighed. "I can't keep this business up and running without Skipper and his boat."

Now all of Woodson's strange behaviors made sense. He wasn't only grieving the loss of his friend but also the loss of his business. Skipper's death might very well destroy Woodson's life.

10

R ebecca flipped the page of the ledger and took another picture. History had taught her to always keep a spare set of evidence when she could. And going through photos of the evidence late at night had often helped her piece together the puzzle that made up every case.

After photographing the entire ledger, she went back to the final excursion logged into the book. Written in what she'd quickly learned was Samuel Graves's scrawl, she made out the name of Lucy Sturgeon booked for June eleventh. The outing included Sturgeon's three daughters and had been booked for the entire day.

There was a signature at the end, verifying the woman had made it back that same date. That clearly hadn't been the trip where he'd gone missing.

Below that entry, a line was smeared, as if someone had erased whatever had been written there. She held the book up to the bright noon sun and tried to read it from every angle but couldn't make out the letters. The back of the page had already been filled out, so she couldn't tell if the pencil had left an imprint there either.

Of course, she only had her eyes, while the techs would be able to find things she couldn't see. She slipped the ledger into an evidence bag and was filling out the label when her radio came on.

"Sheriff, you got your ears on?"

Reaching across her body, she picked up the cruiser radio. "I'm here, Frost. What's up?"

"Forensics is finally finished at the scene and are heading back."

"That will make Vale happy, at least."

"And Viviane was able to find next of kin for Samuel Graves."

"Woodson told me it was Eldridge Graves, an Alzheimer's patient."

"That's what we found. Do you know the name of the facility yet?"

"Not yet. Can you get that?"

"Sure. You busy up there?"

"I got the reservation ledger for Coastal Tours. Graves and Woodson both used it, along with sharing their shop. It has the name of the last person who chartered the boat too. If you have time, can you look that up? I'll put her name in the file."

"Can do. You heading back soon, or you got more to do up there?"

"I'm going to see if I can swing by the police department here to have a chat with Officer Wilson, who supposedly is a real human who has shown up to work at least once to write the missing persons report for Samuel Graves yet did no follow-ups."

There was a pause. "He still hasn't responded?"

"Nope. And I'm done waiting."

❄

NOT ONLY DID the officer in charge of the case not pick up, but when she called dispatch, she found out that Wilson wouldn't be in the office until noon. Rebecca wanted to make good use of her time in Norfolk, so she made a different call.

A call that had been weighing on her mind for nearly a week.

When Robert Leigh had been apprehended after killing three people out of revenge for his daughter's death, he'd been transferred from Southwestern Virginia Mental Health Institute and committed to the psychiatric ward of Norfolk General Hospital. He'd agreed to help Rebecca build her case against the Yacht Club by providing all the information he'd managed to gather.

No time like the present to give the man a visit.

Heading down to the hospital cafeteria while she waited, Rebecca grabbed a doughnut and a fresh cup of coffee. She reviewed the pictures she'd taken, eating with one hand and sorting the images on her phone while taking notes with the other hand.

A man walked up to her table. "Sheriff West?"

She glanced up to find a short man in an expensive suit holding a briefcase and giving her a haughty stare.

"You must be Brandon Gaulding." She closed the image gallery app on her phone and stood.

He flipped a business card over to her. It was heavy stock paper with the name of a prestigious law firm. "I am. You weren't very forthcoming on the phone. Why do you want to see my client? He's in a very delicate state and doesn't need to be unnecessarily disturbed."

"I would rather discuss this with Robert in the privacy of his room."

Gaulding glared at her and wrapped both hands around the handle of his briefcase. "If you want to talk to my client, you have to tell me why first."

Rebecca gave the people around them a pointed look. It was the lunch rush, and there was no chance of privacy. "Not here." She understood that he was only protecting his client, so she softened her tone. "Go tell Robert Leigh that Sheriff Rebecca West is here to see him. Ask him if he wants to see me."

"You haven't tried to see him yet? Or you tried and were turned away?"

"I haven't tried. I wanted you in the room with us first."

That caught him off guard, but he still didn't seem to trust her as he continued to glare. He appeared both intelligent and sharp, something she was pleased to see, just as she was glad to find Robert Leigh in a hospital instead of a jail cell.

"I don't know what you're up to, but I'll talk to my client." He turned and marched off.

She took the time to clear her table, check her phone for messages, and dump her tray. She was waiting outside the psych ward when he came back.

"He wouldn't tell me why but said he's willing to see you."

"Not here." Rebecca smiled, trying to be friendly and open while still being professional. It didn't work.

The attorney made a sound low in his throat. "If you're trying to pull one over on my client, I will sue you, personally, and your office."

She smiled at the threat. "Noted."

He led her down the hall and into a private room. It wasn't a regular hospital room, but looked more like a lounge with a couch, table, and chairs. Robert was sitting at the table, clenching his hands, and his face lit up when Rebecca walked in. Half his hair was white now, including one eyebrow.

A blue robe hung loosely over his frame, and the frayed edges at the cuffs indicated he picked at the fabric.

"Robert, how are you doing?" Rebecca slid into a seat across from him.

He shrugged, and his hand jerked down to his leg. Her heart dropped. He'd made the same movement several times while in custody with her. Any time he became upset, he would reflexively reach for his phone, so he could listen to Cassie's voice message until he calmed down again. She wondered if the doctors had decided not to give it back to him. Just in case, she decided not to bring it up.

His lawyer sat down beside him, resting his briefcase on the table.

"I'm doing okay. The doctors are really helping me." Robert smiled, then stared at his hands as he rubbed his thumbs together. "I have to admit, I'm shocked you showed up."

"I told you I'd stay in touch."

"Have you made any headway?"

His lawyer held up a hand. "What's this about? Are you talking about his case?"

Rebecca glanced around the room, making sure there were no cameras. "You told them you were his lawyer and made sure there are no recording devices here, right?"

Gaulding frowned at her. "Of course I did. I know how to do my job, Sheriff West."

"He's an excellent lawyer. I'm glad you suggested him." Robert smiled, but it faded when she put her finger up to her lips.

"Remember, no one can know I suggested anyone."

Gaulding's frown deepened, and he leaned across the table. "You suggested he use my law firm? Are you admitting my client is innocent, Sheriff West?"

"No, your client is most definitely guilty of those murders." Robert didn't even flinch at the harsh words. "This is about the case of…" She paused because she wasn't sure if she could talk about Cassie without upsetting Robert.

Robert blew out a breath and offered a wobbly smile. "They've got me on some good drugs. It doesn't hurt so much to talk about Cassie anymore. You can say her name."

As brave as he was trying to be, his voice still cracked from the pain. Rebecca reached over and put her hand over his.

Gaulding raised an eyebrow at that.

She pulled her hand back and slipped a sheet of paper out of her bag. Brandon Gaulding moved his arm to stop her from handing it to Robert, but she instead slid it over to him.

"This was the best and safest way I could think of to get you this information. There are no recording devices here, and lawyer-client privilege protects him and you."

"Sheriff, what's this all about?" Gaulding picked up the paper and started reading. "I know some of these names."

"You know them? Or you've heard of them?" Rebecca worried she'd just made a grievous mistake and shared a concerned look with Robert, which the lawyer did not see. She'd checked out Robert's lawyer and had not seen anything that linked him to the Yacht Club or any of the cases thrown out of court for trumped-up reasons.

Gaulding shook his head. "I've read their names in the newspapers and heard about them in town. They're pretty well-known, but they run in much higher circles than I do. A criminal defense attorney like me is well beneath their radar. What do they have to do with my client?" He glared at the paper, then up at Rebecca.

"These are some of the men who might try to come after your client or use their influence on his case."

His eyes narrowed. "Are you threatening my client?"

Robert laughed, and Rebecca smiled but shook her head. She was starting to worry that Robert had not told his lawyer everything about his case. "Not at all. Those are the same men who came after me. Some of them, at least."

Robert jerked back, his eyes frightened. "Wait. Rebecca, they came after you? When?" He reached out his hands but stopped short of touching her as she waved off his concern.

"It was during your case. Don't worry about it. Deputy Frost and I survived."

Robert's eyes began to fill, and she felt like an asshole. She had no idea what kinds of drugs he was on or how they affected his mental health and emotions. "Why didn't you tell me?"

"I didn't want to worry you, Robert. Seriously, don't. We were never really in any danger." She tapped her badge. "Besides, that's my job. Remember? It's my job to stop them. Not yours."

"Don't lie to me. I know what those men can do. We all know."

Gaulding knocked on the table. "Okay, Sheriff, that's enough. You need to tell me what's going on, and you need to tell me now."

"Robert, did you not tell your lawyer about them?"

"Them?" Gaulding looked over at Robert and then back at her.

The man looked embarrassed, but at least he didn't look scared. "No, I wasn't sure who I could trust."

Rebecca squeezed his hand. "I know exactly how you feel. But I've checked him out, and you have to trust someone. You should be able to trust him more than you trust me. And he needs to know what you're up against."

"Can…can you tell him? I still find it so hard to talk about that day."

Rebecca sighed and locked her eyes on him. "I will tell him what I know. But you have to tell him the rest, okay? I only know the most recent parts of this conspiracy."

"Conspiracy?"

Rebecca could tell that Brandon Gaulding was warming to her slightly.

She relented as Robert's eyes pleaded with her. "Okay, I'll start telling the story, but you'll stop me if you start getting too upset? You know this is going to be rough."

Robert's eyes filled with tears again, but he nodded. "Yes."

Reliving his daughter's death and rehashing the details about the men responsible might set back any progress Robert had made. But it was important that his fancy lawyer was aware of the dangers the members of the Yacht Club posed to his client, and possibly to him.

"Okay, Mr. Gaulding, you're going to want to memorize everything you're about to learn and give that list back to me for safekeeping. Your client's life depends on it."

11

Tired of waiting for a call from Officer Wilson, Rebecca headed for the Norfolk Police Department.

She was also frustrated over her inability to have dinner with Ryker last night. When she'd called to ask him if he was available, he'd asked for a raincheck, as he was going to end up working 'til the sun went down. Even after that, he had an indoor job scheduled to replace some windows.

It wasn't Ryker's fault, and she didn't blame him, but it was frustrating when she tried to make inroads into setting down roots in her new town and seemed to get blocked at every turn. Was this another sign she was being a naïve fool? Maybe it was too early to even try. Maybe she should keep things simple, at least for now.

Vale had also sent her an email, complaining about a recent influx of homeless people in town. She had no idea what he was talking about. Some people had been left without a place to stay as buildings and homes were closed for repairs. But even then, it had only been a day, and structures needed to pass inspections before the displaced folks could be moved back in.

Asshole.

She sent him a reply, asking for clarification, and reminded him that being homeless wasn't illegal. And then she'd hopped in her cruiser and left town before he could show up and make a scene.

Before she went inside the Norfolk PD, she checked the shared file again and saw that Officer Wilson still hadn't responded to any of her attempts to reach him. She got out of her cruiser determined that, if Wilson wasn't in, she'd talk to whoever was in charge. His reluctance to work was impairing her ability to do her job. Maybe if she handed him the evidence she'd picked up with just the smallest amount of legwork, that would motivate him to at least do something.

The man at the desk barely even looked up when she walked in.

"Can I help you?"

"I'm here to see Officer Wilson. I'm—"

"Do you have an appointment? Are you here to report a crime?" He talked right over her, still staring at the screen set on his low desk.

I'll get your attention.

"I've got a body he's been looking for in my morgue."

He finally looked up long enough to see the badge she'd pulled from her belt.

"I'm Sheriff West from Shadow Island. If he's still not available, I'll need to speak with his boss. Hopefully, before I have to call in the FBI to coordinate a double homicide that landed on my beach."

His eyes widened before they dulled again and shifted back to his screen. "Wilson doesn't work homicide." He sat there in silence, as if he expected her to do something else, but she just waited. "I'll call him and see what's up."

Rebecca bit back her reflex to thank the man and, instead, crossed her arms over her chest.

The man sighed and picked up the phone. "Wilson, there's a woman here who claims to be a sheriff and wants to talk to you about a body." There was a pause, and Rebecca strained to hear Wilson on the other side of the line but couldn't. "I dunno. Shadow. Never heard of it." Another pause. "Sure." He hung up the phone and pressed a button to unlock the door into the back. "He'll see you."

If this is how the rest of the station is run, I'm not surprised by Wilson's lack of response.

Working with the FBI, Rebecca had been forced to coordinate with all kinds of stations, and one of the things she'd learned first was that the front desk set the mood for the rest of the workforce. If the officers were active and timely, they wouldn't tolerate a slacker out front.

A man in a rumpled uniform was walking toward her before she even made it into the bullpen. His eyes weren't as dull as the dispatcher's, but he did look tired.

"Sheriff West?" He held out his hand.

Rebecca held up her healing palms to indicate she wouldn't be shaking his hand. "That's me. And you're Officer Wilson?"

"Yup. Sorry about not getting back to you before. I got all your messages." He stressed the word "all" and didn't seem in the least bit sorry. In fact, he seemed annoyed as he led her back into the heart of the station. The fact that he hadn't even acknowledged her raw skin told her the man either didn't pay attention to details or simply wanted to be rid of Rebecca as quickly as possible.

"Well, I've got bodies turning to goo in the morgue, and at least one of them is connected to you. He was identified as your missing man. I thought you'd like to know so you could at least close your case. And maybe notify the family."

Officer Wilson shrugged, making it clear he didn't care. "Not really much of a family to tell. I tried to talk to the brother, his only living relative. The man forgot what he was saying as I talked to him and referred to his brother as being in middle school."

"I understand, but you—"

He picked up a folder off his desk. "After the body was identified as a murder victim, I was taken off the case. As a violent crime, it was handed over to Agent Lettinger at VSP over on Center Drive. Good luck."

Without another word, Wilson turned and walked off. Back to sit on his ass and do nothing, or at least that was the vibe he was giving off. The little weasel hadn't even bothered to properly update the missing persons case to the new investigating agency in the NCIC. The National Crime Information Center couldn't coordinate properly with other authorities unless the local agencies kept their files up to date with them.

Even more frustrated now, Rebecca turned on her heels and walked back out to her cruiser, taking the ledger evidence bag she'd brought with her. She looked up the address and was mollified only slightly when she saw how close she was to the Virginia State Police. A few blocks away.

Forcing her mood to lighten from the dark place Wilson had shoved it, Rebecca drove over in a jiff, parked, collected the evidence she'd brought, and walked inside. "If one person tries to blow me off," she muttered under her breath, "I swear I'll turn them to goo myself."

As she stepped inside, a man in uniform looked up with a wary smile. "Can I help you, miss?" His gaze dropped from her face to her waist. "Ah, pardon, Sheriff."

Rebecca smiled, appreciating the effort to get it right. "Yes, I'm here to speak with Agent Lettinger about a case. I've collected some evidence I think he'll need."

The man leaned back, a smile spreading across his face. "Rhonda, you hear that?"

"I heard." A short woman with dirty-blond hair walked out, and Rebecca realized why the dispatcher had only needed to lean back. Lettinger had been standing at the door. "Sheriff West, I hope?"

Rebecca moved to greet the woman, again displaying her palms to indicate she wouldn't be offering a formal greeting. "Yes, and apologies for the 'he.'"

Agent Lettinger nodded at Rebecca's hands. "Should I ask how that happened?"

"Long story about a ladder in the hurricane."

"Sounds interesting. I was going to call you once I got back from my lunch break."

"You haven't eaten yet?" Rebecca glanced at her watch. It was after one o'clock.

"I got busy with work and lost track of time. Say, any chance you like wings?" Lettinger gave her a warm smile that disarmed Rebecca. Her eyes dropped to the bag in Rebecca's hand and her smile wilted. "Oh, you've got evidence. Dammit. Sorry. I'm just starving."

Rebecca's stomach growled. "What kind of wings?"

The warm smile instantly resurfaced. "Whatever kind you want. It's all-you-can-eat wings at Hell's Kitchen tonight, but they cut me some slack and let me come in early. My treat."

"I'm not going to turn down free wings."

"Harry, can you sign for the evidence, please?"

Harry, the man working dispatch, reached out his hand, and Rebecca watched him sign for the bag.

"Let's go." Lettinger pulled her keys out and led Rebecca to her car. After they'd pulled onto the street toward downtown, she asked, "What's in the evidence bag?"

"Samuel Graves's business ledger. It has all the reservations for the last year, including the last one before he disappeared."

"You got it? Wilson didn't?"

"I got it. I have no idea what Wilson has done other than tell me to come see you."

Lettinger sighed as she maneuvered to park on the street next to a narrow, single door. *Hell's Kitchen* glowed in red neon in the large front window. On the other side of the glass, a long wooden bar was adorned with racks of alcohol.

"That doesn't surprise me."

"Is this a bar?" Rebecca stepped out of the car and up onto the sidewalk.

"At night. Virginia is funny. Bars have to serve meals too. And this is one of the best in the area, so they're open for lunch as well. I've never been here on a weekend night, but I hear they're always packed."

Lettinger held the door open for her, and a woman with short brown hair and double tattoo sleeves glanced up as they walked in. Her eyes lit up as the agent entered.

"Rhonda, you want your usual?" The restaurant was larger than Rebecca had expected in such an old building. A wall that had once separated the two shop fronts had been removed, and the other section was filled with tables and chairs.

"You know it." She waved toward the two raised booths in front of the door.

Rebecca slid into the black, leather booth. "Virginia does have some interesting laws."

"Oh, yeah, it does." Lettinger laughed and slid a menu over to her. "Check out their drink section. They do all kinds of flavored lemonades."

Rebecca's mouth watered. "And flavored teas, too, I see, but lemonade sounds exactly like what I need today."

Lettinger grinned, her brown eyes huge in her heart-shaped face. "You drove out here to discuss the Samuel Graves case, right?"

"Yup. You know anything about it?"

The bartender walked up then and set a yellow-green glass down in front of Lettinger. "And what can I get you, darling?"

"Raspberry lemonade sounds good."

"And since you're here with Rhonda, I'm guessing you want wings too?"

"Uhm…" Rebecca scanned the menu. "I'll have the Old Bay wings."

"Alrighty. I'll leave you two to your work."

Lettinger waited until she disappeared behind the bar before answering Rebecca's question. "I was just assigned to it yesterday, so I'm barely caught up. Far as I know, Samuel Graves, aka Skipper, went missing along with his boat a few weeks ago. Since then, no one's had any sighting of him. He's got a business associate who reported him missing because Skipper didn't have anyone else in his life who noticed he was gone. He wasn't a loner, just managed to outlive most of his friends and family except his brother, who's in assisted living and can't remember much of anything."

Rebecca nodded. "That's what I've learned too."

"While doing some fishing after the hurricane, someone found Graves's body on your beach on Shadow Island along with another body. I haven't read the autopsy report yet. Do you have anything more to add to that?"

"Autopsy isn't in yet. M.E. will make sure you get a copy of the results as soon as they're available."

"I sort of assumed there would just be skeletal remains."

"I was surprised, too, that there was anything left when I learned how long Skipper had been missing. We did find tiny remnants of blue plastic on one of them. The M.E. guessed they were wrapped up in a tarp before they were dumped, so the larger scavengers couldn't feast until the tarp ripped in the storm and the bodies became exposed. It's just a guess, but our medical examiner is top-notch. I'm hopeful her report will fill in some of the gaps."

They both waited as the server came back and dropped off two large plates of wings, with cups of sauces, celery, and Rebecca's drink. Without a word, she turned and walked off again, letting them continue their working lunch. Her actions made it clear this wasn't the first time Rhonda had come here to work and eat.

"The ledger I brought to you. Can you have your forensic team look over it?" Rebecca took a long drink of her lemonade.

"Of course. What should I tell them to look for?"

"After the last paid excursion, there's an entry that appears to be erased."

"And you want them to try and pull out what was written there?"

Rebecca appreciated the instant rapport she felt with the agent. *Competent and insightful.* "Exactly. It could be nothing."

"Not a problem. I'll get them on that as soon as I return to the office."

They fell into an amicable silence and dug into their plates.

"You know, another theory is that they were killed recently." Lettinger wiped her hands on a paper napkin.

"Another possibility," Rebecca agreed. "Do you have any idea who the second body might be?" She took a bite of her spiced wing, careful to keep the sauce off the tender new skin on her hands. A low moan escaped her lips as the savory sauce washed over her tongue.

"It's good, right? I told you they were the best. Try it with the blue cheese. I can check the local database of missing people to see if we can get a match after the autopsy is done."

Rebecca took the agent's advice and dunked her wing into the creamy mixture. "But with the boat missing as well, and considering where they were found, Skipper could have picked up the other party anywhere."

Lettinger blew out a breath and dropped a bone to the table. "That's true."

Rebecca licked her thumb, wincing at the sting in a wound. "The Atlantic Ocean is a big place."

Lettinger picked up another wing, looking about as forlorn as Rebecca felt. "We're looking for a needle in a needle field that's been flooded."

Rebecca smiled, but the gesture didn't hold. "Yeah. And it's filled with sharks."

12

"Hey, Darian, got a call out for you." Melody spun around in her chair and waved a piece of paper at him.

Darian Hudson closed the most recent file on the shared drive of his computer and sighed. He still wasn't caught up on all the cases that had been opened and closed in the last couple weeks. It wasn't required, but he always felt better when he knew the lay of the land when it came to the job. That used to be easy, but now it was getting hectic ever since a certain sheriff arrived.

Which was fine by him.

"What's it about?" He pulled his gun out of his drawer and placed it in his holster before locking down his workstation.

"Got a drunk-and-disorderly at Shoreline Tavern."

He sighed with relief, then realized how strange that was. But at least he wasn't going to need backup to handle this. Both Hoyt and Rebecca had finished their shifts. The idea of calling on Locke gave him the heebie-jeebies. The man was just too unreliable and as likely to escalate a situation as calm one.

Rebecca walked up from the back as they were talking, carrying her laptop bag and travel mug.

"Hey, Sheriff, wanna head over to a D-and-D at the tavern? Should be fun. You haven't had one of those yet, have you?"

Her shoulders slumped, and she glanced at the mug in her hand. "I was hoping to get home and eat a real meal in my own house for once."

He batted his eyelashes at her. "You're going to make me do this all on my own?"

Guilt became a living thing on her face. "Do you actually need help, or…?"

Darian laughed and waved her off, heading to the front. "Nah, I'm totally just messing with you. I don't have anything else I need to deal with, and this should be a simple show up, yell at someone, and maybe write a ticket. If it was anything big, the bartender there would have tossed them out with a broken nose and would have called for an assault."

"If it changes, page me, and I'll come help out. If not, don't call me. At all. Or text." She kept moving to the door, her smile growing with each step.

That hopeful look in Rebecca's eye and the way she kept moving away made him think she was hoping for more than a quiet, solo dinner, but she was out the door before he could come up with a way to razz her about her possible plans with a certain handyman.

"I'll head on over. Melody, tell them I'm on my way."

"Will do. Holler if you need anything."

Melody handed over the form, and he took it as he walked out to his cruiser.

It was still a nice evening as Darian started his cruiser and headed to the tavern. The normal chirps of birds and frogs were chased off by the sounds of hammers and power tools. In a way, it was just as natural to him, though. He watched the flurry of activity as people worked faster to beat the lowering sun.

The animals were moving back in and rebuilding their homes, and so were the humans. Most of them were building back better too. No matter what happened, humans always rebuilt. Especially the ones who lived on his island. They were strong and resilient.

Darian's eyes widened at the sight of the brilliant teal paint being rolled onto the freshly patched walls of Hugh's Surf Shop. Okay, maybe not everything was better.

He pulled his gaze away before the neon paint burned his retinas and focused on driving. Shoreline Tavern wasn't far away, so they didn't usually have any issues there, because of its proximity to the station. But when they did, any ruckus was shut down quickly.

While most places catered to tourists, this one was more low-key. A bar that served simple food, had a small dance floor, and a few pool tables. Being dinnertime, and the fact that they were known for the best burgers in town, parking was limited, so Darian pulled up to the front door instead. It would make it easier to get in and out if he had to drag someone along with him.

He opened the door and held it as a couple walked out laughing, chased out by loud and off-key singing.

"He's in the back at the pool tables." A woman sitting at the bar turned to face him. It was Kelly Hunt, a local. Brody, her golden retriever, was by her side. The normally happy dog lay on his side, a paw covering his exposed ear. "Have fun with that."

"Is it the songbird back there?" He flinched as the singer tried to carry a pitch higher than he could manage and strangled it instead.

"Oh yeah. Can't miss him."

Darian walked inside and followed the horrible singing,

along with the pointing of every staff member who saw him. As if the crowd of people staring and laughing and taking videos on their phones wasn't enough, he could see the man above the crowd.

The guy, thirties, was standing topless on a pool table, singing his heart out while whirling his shirt around his head. He was jerking around in what might be a dance, except he was wearing work boots on the felt-lined surface while trying to avoid the hanging lights.

Logan Ashford shook his shoulders, belting out "Man I Feel Like a Woman," making his big belly shake over his belt, and causing a few people in the crowd to cheer.

"He jumped up there when we told him he couldn't dance between the tables and to take it to the dance floor." A server had followed Darian over and glared at the drunk patron. "I told him that was his last beer, and he was cut off. Then he said he was going out with an encore. As if that makes any sense. First name's Logan. That's all I got."

"Yeah, yeah, I recognize him now. Drunk logic, gotta love it." Darian chuckled and pushed his way through the crowd.

As soon as they saw him, people started moving out of his way—a few even applauded. Unfortunately, Logan thought they were applauding him, so he knocked his beer back and sang even louder.

"Men's pricks, short dicks. Go wild! My style. Color my bear, whaddya care. Whoo, whoo, I love being free!"

Shania Twain's song continued playing in the background with the real lyrics, but that didn't affect Logan, as he was making up his own.

"Okay, Logan, you've butchered the song enough. Time to get down." Darian waved both hands in the air.

The drunk noticed the deputy for the first time. "Darian! Hey, man, did you come to dance with me?" He swung his shirt around again and thrust his hips. "Feeling a woman!"

"You're going to be feeling like hammered spam tomorrow if you don't put that beer down and start drinking some electrolytes." Darian kept the grin on his face to keep Logan calm.

He was generally a happy drunk but could turn to weeping or cursing if provoked. Right now, everyone was amused or just slightly annoyed at their dinners being interrupted, and Darian didn't want things to turn sour.

"That's for tomorrow's Logan to worry about." He slurred and shook his finger at a spot just to the left of Darian. "So don't you go harshing today's Logan with that nonsense. 'Cause today is special."

"What's so special about today, Logan?"

"It's my anniversary!" Logan threw his arms over his head and danced around, shuffling his boots over the felt of the table.

"Then you should be celebrating it with your woman, and not here tearing up a perfectly nice pool table."

"Ha!" Logan bent in half, faking a laugh in Darian's direction. "Ha ha, you're so funny! I'm not celebrating her. I'm celebrating my divorce. She can't tell me what to do no more!"

As Darian watched, the jubilance faded away from Logan, and his attention turned back to the bottle in his hand. "So I'm having a beer at the end of a hard day and dancing with my friends. Because it's the Fourth of July and that's when we celebrate our freedoms. Whoo!"

"It's not the Fourth, Logan."

"Christmas in July, then!" Logan suckled on the empty bottle and didn't notice he wasn't drinking anything.

"The Fourth of July is also about fireworks, and unless you wanna see some fireworks, you're going to get down from that table right now."

"Aww, man, why are you harshing my buzz, man?" Logan pouted.

"Because that's my favorite pool table, and you're tearing it up."

Logan stopped his dancing and looked down at his boots. "Oh. Shit. Sorry, man. Yeah. Can't fuck up the table."

Darian had to reach up and catch Logan as the man clumsily lowered himself down with exaggerated care. There were chuckles around them as people went back to their own business now that the show was over.

The server nodded to Darian and mouthed a *thank you*.

"If…uh, if I fucked up the velvet, tell them to put it on my tab." Logan burped, swayed, and dizzily looked around. Then he carefully set his empty bottle down on thin air and smiled at Darian.

It hit the floor and bounced.

"I'll do that, Logan. How about we get you some water?"

The drunk man smacked his lips a few times and nodded. "That sounds like a good plan. And maybe something to eat. I haven't had dinner yet."

"I know just the place." Darian led the man through the amused crowd as Logan struggled to pull his shirt on again. "It has food, water, and a nice cot to sleep on."

"Oh, that sounds nice."

"It's so nice, it even has a name." Darian led them out of the tavern and opened the back door of the cruiser.

"Really? What is it?" Logan gave him wide eyes as he dropped onto the seat and struggled to stay upright.

"We call it the drunk tank. And it's just for you." Darian closed the door with a laugh at Logan's shocked face.

13

For the second time in two days, Rebecca was home before nine p.m. She could get used to this.

Nothing else could be done with the investigation until the autopsy was back, and Lettinger was combing through the missing persons files for a match with their second vic, so Rebecca didn't even have to worry about that. She thought she had tracked down the last customer Skipper had, but she was waiting for a call back to confirm. Until then, she could relax.

And for the second time in a row, she'd called Ryker and found him busy, prepping a different site for the fireworks display.

She got to sit on her back porch, sip a cup of hot coffee, and watch the evening sun glint off the water. But she was doing it alone. Her omelet with fresh-chopped veggies had been delicious, but it would have tasted better if she'd had company while she ate it.

A dog running on the beach caught her attention, and she wondered if Ryker had gotten out earlier than expected. But then the dog drew closer, and she saw it wasn't Humphrey running up to her. It was Brody with his owner, who was chasing after him. Kelly Hunt was yelling at the golden retriever, but he was far too overstimulated by all the new smells on the beach to listen.

Rebecca broke off a piece of her dinner, making sure it was only eggs, and whistled loudly.

Intrigued by the new sound, Brody looked over. When he saw her holding her hand out, he came trotting over to see what was being offered.

"You like eggs? I bet you do! Here ya go. Have some." She held her hand down with her palm open.

Drool was already dripping from Brody's lips as he trundled up the steps to the elevated back deck, trailing his leash behind him. He snuffled into her hand, then snatched up the egg, swallowed, and started licking her palm in search of more.

"Greedy boy, maybe you would've enjoyed it more if you'd actually chewed it." Rebecca laughed and ruffled his ears.

The pooch sat down, and his eyes closed partway as she worked her nails along his skull, down his neck, and took hold of his leash. If he noticed, he didn't mind, so long as she kept scratching his ears.

"Do you want some more?"

Brody's eyes shot open and locked onto her plate. Slobber started to leak out again. Rebecca laughed and moved her feet out from under him.

Kelly came jogging up to the porch, huffing and puffing. "Oh, Rebecca, I'm so sorry. He caught me off guard and just took off running to chase the birds. I couldn't keep up."

"It's totally okay."

Brody wagged his tail and hopped up to greet his owner.

"Yeah, you act like a sweetheart in front of company. Why can't you be a good boy all the time?"

"Don't worry about it. I was just sitting here thinking how nice it would be to have some company."

Kelly's smile disappeared. "Are you okay? Anything wrong?"

Rebecca waved her off with a laugh. "No, I was only thinking dinner tastes better when you have someone to share it with. Then Brody showed up hungry."

"Brody is always hungry, if you're willing to share food. And, also, if you're *not* willing to share." Kelly motioned at the empty second chair. "If you're wanting company, I'd be happy to sit down for a while."

"That would be lovely. Would you like something to drink? I've got red wine, coffee stout, coffee, and water."

"A red wine would be wonderful." Kelly sank into the chair and took over the leash for Rebecca as she got up to fetch the beverage. "How are you settling in here? I haven't talked to you in a few weeks, but it seems to me that everything has changed for you."

That's an understatement.

Rebecca laughed and thought back to where she had been when she'd first met Kelly. It had been right here, but then, she had just moved in. She handed her a glass and sat back down.

"Well, as I'm sure you've heard, I didn't get to start my vacation."

Kelly laughed and sipped the wine. "I heard. The day after I met you, Sheriff Wallace showed up at your door, right?"

"Right. And things haven't slowed down since."

"That's good. There was a town meeting about it. Well, it wasn't on the agenda, but it still came up. Everyone was all for voting you in after Hoyt Frost said you had his endorsement."

Rebecca's eyebrows shot up. "Hoyt said that?"

Kelly's eyes widened with glee. "Oh yeah, he did. Was

quite eloquent about it as well. There was no way the Select Board wouldn't offer you the interim position after that."

So Vale really didn't do me any favors. He did himself *a favor so he wouldn't look bad.*

"You know, I came down here because I thought it was going to be so much different from D.C. But it's really not. It's the same ole same ole, just on a smaller scale."

That feeling of homesickness accompanied by sadness and grief over loss, *hiraeth* she'd learned it was called from her mother, was still not sated.

"One of my first memories is of sitting on the beach here, watching the Fourth of July fireworks with my parents. We'd take a blanket down and have a picnic dinner. The fireworks would shoot up over the water, and it was like watching them twice because of their reflection in the ocean. I never figured out how you guys did that. Made it look like it was shooting out of the water."

Kelly laughed. "I take it you never watched them as an adult. If you had, it would have been obvious." At Rebecca's headshake, Kelly laughed again. "We shoot them off from the water. All the fireworks are loaded up onto boats, driven out, and set off in patterns."

It was so obvious Rebecca joined her in her laughter. "Of course. Why did I never think of that?"

"Memory is a funny thing. From your perspective as a child," she held her hand about three feet from the ground, "it probably did look like it was coming from the water. And after that, you saw what you expected."

"I can't believe my parents never corrected me." Rebecca shook her head at her own silly bias that had kept her from seeing reality. "Still, I'm even more impressed now that I know more about fireworks. It would take an engineer to figure out the calculations and planning."

"But it's so worth it." Kelly smiled out at the ocean. "It's one of my favorite times of the year."

"This will be my first time seeing them again since I lost my parents." Rebecca hadn't meant to say that part out loud. The bitter truth had just slipped out of her mouth.

"Is it going to be hard on you? You can come watch them with me if you want. If you don't want to be alone."

Rebecca's phone buzzed, and she looked down at it. It was a text from Ryker. She opened it.

Vale has us moving everything over to Sand Dollar Beach and we're going to work from sunup to sundown to get it done. My raincheck will last long enough, right?

She tapped back a quick *yes* with an old-school smiley face and looked up at Kelly. From the look on the other woman's face, she knew she'd failed to hide her disappointment in the message she'd just received. She tucked the phone back in her pocket.

"Where will you and Brody be watching from?"

"Down at the beach with Angie Frost and that gang."

Rebecca stroked the dog's soft fur. "I'll do my best to be there too."

14

W ith a sense that her case was no longer going to be sandbagged by incompetent officers, Rebecca walked into the office. Viviane must have needed to run an errand because Hoyt was sitting at the dispatch desk.

He gave her a brief nod. "Morning, Boss. Get your errands in Norfolk done yesterday?"

She rolled her eyes and headed back to get a coffee refill. "That idiot Wilson is no longer on the case. Which is fine since he didn't bother to do more than the initial report. It was handed over to the state police."

Hoyt snorted. "Is that agent doing anything?"

"Thankfully, yes. Agent Rhonda Lettinger just received it halfway through her shift yesterday, but she's already got a better handle on it than Wilson ever did."

With a fresh cup, she came back and leaned against the counter. She caught Hoyt staring at her hands.

"What?"

"Where are your bandages?"

"Skin heals better when it can breathe, Mom. I'm fine." She was touched by his genuine concern but waved it off by refocusing the conversation. "I gave Lettinger the reservation ledger I collected from the shop. Wilson never even bothered to go down and check that out."

Hoyt allowed her to pivot. "Speaking of the ledger, I looked up the last customer Graves had. There's no Lucy Sturgeon in Virginia with daughters. She must have been from out of town. Did you have anything else to go on?"

"Not really. Wilson didn't bother following up on her. I've got a picture of Lucy and her three girls, though. I might be able to get some information once we get the banking records, if she paid with a card or check."

"And what about the unidentified body?"

Rebecca rubbed her temple. "Lettinger and I talked about that too. She's going to search through the local database of missing people and find the males who went missing around the same time, trying to match the estimated height range of the other vic. But after that, we'll have to wait for the autopsy to give us some more details to see if there's a possible link to one of them. With the state they were in, I'm not going to make a guess at anything like weight or age."

"Well, that should be fun. Did you learn anything else?"

"His boat is missing. The *Chum Runner*."

Hoyt looked across the desk with a raised eyebrow.

Rebecca lifted both hands in self-defense. "Hey, that's a whole lot better than the *Tide Bagger* or *Mermaid's Clam*. It still bothers me those entitled Yacht Club idiots choose such vulgar names for their boats."

"Yachts," he said, with a semi-straight face.

She rolled her eyes before continuing. "The *boat* went missing the same day Graves did. We need to put that into the file and look for it too." She took a sip of her coffee, enjoying the calm and quiet of the office for once.

"Coast Guard is our best chance for that."

"Would've been nice if the Norfolk PD had asked them to

start looking two weeks ago." She just didn't understand the lackadaisical attitude. "I understand they're a naval base town with a lot of people moving in and out. But when they have a case with a long-standing local, you would think they'd at least do something."

"Not gonna lie, cops like that are the reason I moved back here and took a job as a deputy. Places like that, the cops get worn out so fast they can only keep up with the paperwork." He shook his head, swiveling back and forth in the chair. "As soon as they have a chance to fob it off to someone else, they do. They don't start, follow through, and wrap up cases like we do here."

That made a lot of sense. She'd seen the same thing in the FBI. Especially missing persons cases. After the initial rush of putting the case together, it became a wait-and-see operation. Still, Wilson hadn't done any bit of investigation, and that was what annoyed her.

"Then I guess it's a good thing those victims landed on our beach instead of somewhere else. Despite the fact that we seem to have had a slew of them recently."

"Maybe it would make you feel better to know that there are still regular minor crimes happening too."

"Yeah? Did I miss something?"

"Happened last night. It's already filed, but I'm sure you haven't had a chance to see it. A nice, simple, nonviolent drunk-and-disorderly."

"Oh, that's where Darian was off to when I slipped out. He was razzing me and making me think he needed my assistance. I was starting to think there wasn't any crime in this town except the big ones."

Hoyt chuckled. "Thankfully, we've got Logan Ashford to remind us that things aren't always extreme."

"What did this Logan character do?"

"He had a few too many last night while, and I quote, 'celebrating being free from his ex-wife.' Their divorce was finalized yesterday."

Rebecca laughed. She'd heard of divorce parties, but this was the first time she'd heard of throwing a one-person divorce party. The first year after she'd split from her ex hadn't been fun, but life was so much better now.

"I'm betting we'll get more than a few of those this holiday weekend."

"Oh yeah, we will. Logan's already woken up, learned to regret his drinking, and gotten a taxi home. Since we're not set up with a drunk tank or holding cell, we have to run them to the mainland. We have a deal with Coastal Ridge PD. If we handle the initial paperwork for the citation, they house 'em for the night and handle the case from there."

Rebecca still couldn't believe the department didn't have any kind of holding cell. The reality of that deficiency had been abundantly clear when she was forced to hold Malcolm Jenner in a near-catatonic state in the interrogation room as the hurricane bore down on the island.

One more thing to figure out if I stay on as sheriff.

"I called over to Coastal Ridge first thing, and they told me Logan had been released. Darian gave him the citation for it already. It's all sorted, and a copy is on your desk if you want to read it over."

She grinned. "Since you conned me into this sheriff job, I kind of have to."

Hoyt opened his mouth to respond but snapped it closed when the door opened, and Richmond Vale came stalking in. He was already glowering. Or maybe he was still glowering. Rebecca tried to remember a time when he wasn't scowling at someone.

"Morning, Mr. Vale. Is this an official visit, or—"

"This is all your fault!" He tried to slam the door, but it opened outward and was on a hydraulic closer, so nothing happened. "We had to find a new place to set up for the Fourth of July fireworks because of that mess on the beach!"

Rebecca looked at Hoyt, who shrugged and said nothing.

She sighed. "First, I'd like to know what you're accusing me of. Are you suggesting I killed two men? Or just that I found the dead bodies in the aftermath of a hurricane and hauled them onto the beach? Or are you saying I am Hurricane Boris?" She wanted to put some snark in her voice, but his accusation was just too confusing.

Hoyt had a sudden coughing fit that he covered with a fist.

Vale's scowl deepened. "You know what I'm talking about."

"No." Rebecca shook her head. "I really don't. What do you think I did that would in any way impact where the fireworks are set up? Our crime scene is clear. The tape has already come down. The media is focusing on the Norfolk murder aspect, not where the victims were found. The beach is clear, and the sand raked smooth without any traces left. What more do you want?"

His glare got so intense she wondered if the vein in his neck might pop. She hoped so and didn't feel a bit guilty for the wish.

"We have an invasion of homeless people who need to be cleared out!"

Rebecca tried to keep up with the sudden change in subject and glanced at Hoyt. He had his coughing under control but looked as baffled as she felt.

"Other than Mac, who is already on his way to a shelter, who else are you talking about?"

Vale stomped his foot. "Just get rid of them!"

"There are several homes that were damaged in the storm and can't be occupied right now. Are you suggesting that we arrest people for having storm damage and no other place to sleep? Or just arrest everyone at the FEMA camps? Because I think the Feds would take serious exception to that idea. Also, that would be illegal for us to even try." Rebecca was tired of Vale's bullshit and didn't hide her disdain.

Hoyt stepped in. "Look, Vale, once the windows and wall at the hostel are fixed, everyone can go back to their rooms."

Vale's glare didn't even shift from Rebecca, boring into her. "You know, I thought you would be a lot more accommodating after we got you into this position."

Rebecca bit back her ire, digging her fingernails into her tender palms to keep from taking the arrogant man's head off. "While I *appreciate* the job, I have a sworn duty to uphold the law, not follow your ideas of what should be done in town. I'm the sheriff, not a queen. I have to follow the laws just like everyone else."

He didn't seem to have a response to that and, instead, spun on his heel and stormed out the door.

Rebecca pressed her knuckles into her forehead. "He does know he's not my boss, right?"

Hoyt barked out a laugh. "Probably not. He thinks he's the boss of everyone."

15

Rebecca inhaled the aroma of fresh coffee as Viviane returned to the office with the caffeinated elixir.

"Morning, Boss!" Viviane looked especially chipper today, dressed in a red, white, and blue checkered shirt. "I was feeling festive and decided to grab everyone some java."

"That was very kind of you." Rebecca poked her head out of the bullpen. "How's your morning been so far?"

"Pretty quiet, thank goodness." Viviane placed the coffee carrier on the dispatch desk and waved a memo sheet. "Can you hand this to Hoyt on your way through. It's his note about that Lucy woman he was trying to locate earlier."

Hoyt rolled over in his chair, looking completely relaxed. "Do I hear someone talking about me?"

"Only truthful things. Like how you're always eavesdropping and sticking your nose where it doesn't belong." Viviane smiled, showing most of her teeth.

"I am a deputy. That's kind of my job." He waved his hand around. "And this is the office. It's hard not to eavesdrop."

Rebecca handed the note to her deputy. "You found our

Lucy Sturgeon?" Rebecca walked while sipping her coffee, and Hoyt rolled along with her.

Hoyt thumped his forehead with his palm. "Oh, yeah. Sorry. Should have led with that." He waved the note. "Found her, and she definitely remembered going on that excursion. Said it was a ton of fun getting to see the Virginia coastline. And she couldn't say enough good things about Skipper."

"Did she remember anything suspicious? Anything unusual? Or see anyone who seemed angry with Skipper?" She inhaled the contents of her cup and turned to face him.

"Just the opposite. She said Skipper was a friendly guy who cracked jokes, told stories, and kept them entertained the whole trip. He shared some fun history about the area, though she said it sounded like some of it was made up to entertain them." He checked his notes. "Talked with everyone on the dock, coming and going. He even gave them suggestions for where to go next, or get dinner, talked about all the amazing mom-and-pop run businesses where they would get good value for their money."

"So no enemies but a ton of friends and work acquaintances. That's what I learned too. It seems like everyone loved him."

"That was Lucy's impression too. She was despondent to hear he had died. And had no idea who would want to do such a thing to a 'sweet gentleman like him.'" Hoyt air-quoted the last few words. "According to her, his trip was the highlight of their vacation, and her kids couldn't stop talking about him."

Rebecca sighed. "I keep hoping to find some downside to him, some reason a person might want him dead. But he seemed to be a legitimately good guy."

"Maybe he was in the wrong place at the wrong time?"

"Or took the wrong guy out on his boat."

"You mean the other dead guy?"

She shrugged and pulled out her phone. "Or the trip that was supposed to happen after Lucy's…but got erased."

"After? I thought she was the last one."

"The last one we had a name for." Flipping the phone, she showed him the pictures she'd taken of the ledger. "The line under hers was smudged, as if someone had a reservation, but then it was erased."

"Or they took the reservation and came back later to destroy the evidence." He moved the picture to inspect the sign-in box. "I can't tell if this was filled out and erased or not."

"Neither could I. Agent Lettinger is going to have her lab examine it. If there's anything there, they'll find it."

Hoyt rubbed his chin. "What about a computer? Could they have kept digital copies?"

"Not one that I saw. They had a stack of papers behind the desk that Woodson was going through when I walked in. He said he had to close up his business. I checked the metadata for his website. An outside company runs it. Not Woodson or Graves."

"Does anyone actually use just pen and paper anymore, though? I mean, I'm an old fart, and I still file my taxes online."

Rebecca grinned but managed not to laugh. "Well, they're older farts than you. Or maybe they're just technophobes. Who knows? I'm still waiting on Skipper's bank records. When I get them, I might find some answers in there. But at this point, I'm betting on it being the other man."

Viviane piped up. "Or pirates."

They both turned to look at her.

She shrugged, as if it should be an obvious answer. "Let's say two men went out on a boat. No schedule, so we didn't know where they were going. And no one saw them after they left their slip. They probably went out to deep waters. International waters. A boat nice enough to run as a charter would be nice enough to catch the eye of pirates, especially if Skipper's was as well-known and profitable as she sounds."

Rebecca studied her friend. "Good point."

"Charter boats deal in a lot of cash. Only the reservations are made with cards." Viviane brought her hands together like she was closing a book. "High-value target with money on board mysteriously went missing, all hands on deck found dead, and it happened in late spring when there isn't a lot of other traffic to catch them. That sounds like pirates to me."

Rebecca looked at Hoyt, who shrugged and tilted his head. She nodded.

"It could be pirates," Rebecca agreed, thinking all the possibilities through. "If that's what happened, it will most likely be a Coast Guard case. I'll see if we've had an uptick in pirate activity nearby, or if they've heard of any specific ones."

Hoyt tapped his keyboard to wake up his monitor. "I'll call up some of my buddies and see if they've seen any suspicious boats in the area. Other than the normal ones."

That line made Rebecca wonder if this was related to the Yacht Club. But Skipper had left port in Norfolk. While that was close enough to drive to, it was out of the presumed comfort zone where most of the Yacht Club roamed. They preferred waters that were less traveled by the Navy and Coast Guard, both of whom had bases in Norfolk.

And a law enforcement unit that looks the other way.

Or used to.

"That gives us plenty to look into while we wait on Bailey and the VSP techs. Viviane, if this pans out, I'll pick you up one of your favorite milkshakes."

Viviane lifted her arms in the air, touchdown style. "Pirates for the win!"

Rebecca also made a mental note to check into the known local patterns for them. The last thing she wanted was for the tourists flocking to the area to put themselves in danger as they sailed in for the Fourth of July celebration.

16

"Found anything yet, Frost?"

After an excellent start to her morning, Rebecca had grown tired and slightly cranky from staring at her screen with no results. She hoped her deputy had gotten luckier.

Hoyt met her eyes from where he was slumped on his desk, looking just as bleak as she felt. "Not yet. Some maybes, but nothing even worth checking into. How's your search going?"

She shook her head and kept walking through the bullpen for the door. "Slow and dull. I'm going to pop out for an early lunch. Hopefully, that will help wake me up."

"Food. That reminds me. Angie wanted me to tell you you're invited to join us for our barbecue on the beach."

That got her attention. "Barbecue? When?"

"On the Fourth. When everyone is going to be barbecuing on the beach. To celebrate Independence Day." He shook his head. "You really must be hungry if you forgot about that."

"I'm hungry enough that you just talking about food knocked all thought out of my head. Any chance that Angie is going to be making her cheesy noodles for it?" She licked her lips just remembering the taste of Angie Frost's famous baked five-cheese macaroni.

Hoyt laughed. "There's a good chance that if I told her about your hopeful expression, she'd be happy to make cheesy noodles for you."

Rebecca's stomach growled at the thought. "Then count me in."

"I'll tell her to make extra." He waved her off. "Go get your lunch before your stomach eats your spine."

"Yeah, Boss." She chuckled, walked out the front, and turned to head to the parking lot.

Rebecca stopped as Ryker's truck pulled up to the curb.

He rolled down a window. "Let me guess. You were just leaving to take care of something and are in a hurry?"

Rebecca was surprised to see him and wasn't sure what to say at first. What could he be doing here in the middle of the day like this? "Actually, I'm not in any real rush. I was heading out for my lunch break."

His eyes lit up. "Does that mean you have some free time?"

Pleased to her core, she nodded. "At least an hour. Do you have something in mind?"

"How do you feel about fish tacos?" Ryker indicated a bag on his passenger seat.

"I love fish tacos."

"They're from Seafood Shack. They're catering the main event party at Sand Dollar Beach this weekend. We just finished setting up their outdoor market, so we got some of the test batch. And I've got an hour for a break too."

She looked around. "I'm guessing the beach is out as a good place to eat. But there's a breakroom in the back. We can eat there, if you want."

It was a really lame place for a lunch date, but it was

better than nothing. And it was the best she could do on such short notice.

And as soon as I walk in there with him, it will open me up to all kinds of teasing from Hoyt and Viviane.

"Let me park, and I'll be right back."

Less than a minute later, he was by her side. Since he was carrying a bag, Rebecca opened the door, and he walked in ahead of her.

"Well, hey, Ryker, what are you doing…oh. I see."

Rebecca could nearly see Viviane's catty little tail twitching with curiosity as she stepped up around Ryker. "Looks like I'm dining in today."

"Enjoy." Viviane pushed the button to unlock the half door.

Hoyt looked up as Rebecca led Ryker down the hallway. He waved, and Ryker waved back. Rebecca braced herself for the razzing she would get for the rest of the week. She glanced back and saw the smile on Ryker's face. It would be worth it.

The lounge in the back was rarely used, but it had a comfortable couch and a coffee table. She walked in and sat down on the far side of the sofa.

Ryker paused, glanced around for another chair, then sat down next to her. He opened the bag and pulled out several sleeves of tacos, then cups of condiments, and some sides. There was guacamole, salsa, sour cream, and two dishes of black beans. He pushed one of the sleeves over to her and motioned to dig in.

"So. How's work going?" She mentally groaned at the weak conversation starter, but he didn't seem to mind.

"Aggravating." He rolled his eyes before taking a bite of his food.

"Vale?" He seemed the likely source of frustration.

Ryker grunted. "Can you believe that man insists we prioritize the tourist areas over the residential ones?"

Rebecca added salsa and sour cream to her taco before folding it back up. "He blamed me for needing to move the fireworks setup because of the dead bodies on the beach. So yeah, I completely believe it." She took a bite of the flaky, fried white fish hanging over the edge of the corn tortilla. "I have to admit, I don't understand how that man is in an elected position."

Ryker stopped chewing and swallowed hard. "That's an excellent question."

"I mean, I've not been here long, but I've never seen any good come from Vale that wasn't forced. And he seems to be a bully. Giving a bully any kind of power is just asking for problems. Putting them in charge of other people in ways that deal with their money or safety could lead to a disaster."

His eyebrows scrunched together. "I never pictured you as someone who cared about politics."

Rebecca didn't want to admit that the source of her concern came from how poorly Vale treated Ryker. "One of the weird aspects of being a sheriff, I have to at least pay atten-tion to the politics." She took a bite and thought as she chewed. "I never thought I would care either. But then, I never thought I'd be anything more than a tourist lounging on my back deck."

He smiled and grabbed a spoonful of beans. "Are you really saying that working as a sheriff in a small town is more political than working for the FBI in the country's capital?"

She nodded. "That was something the bigwigs had to do. Not anything I had to deal with." As the words left her mouth, she realized that wasn't true. In fact, the last two years of her job were choked out by politics, which was why she'd left. It was also the reason she'd ended up shot and bleeding out in a parking garage.

Her shoulder twinged, and she rotated it out of habit, reaching to massage it and wincing as her raw palm scraped across the seam of her shirt.

"You okay? I heard you'd taken a bit of a beating during the hurricane. Is it still bothering you?"

She realized what she was doing and stopped, picking up her food again. "No, my hands are healing. Sometimes I just forget they need a little extra babying."

His expression filled with concern. "I can see they're healing. I meant the shoulder. That was probably more serious."

"It's an old injury."

Ryker raised his eyebrows.

Rebecca took that as a sign to continue. She lowered her voice, hoping the conversation would remain in the lounge. "When I was in the FBI, I did end up getting sucked into politics." She swallowed hard and leaned back on the couch. "I was tracking down an organized crime group and started taking heat from people higher up in the agency. Then I was told to back off. I didn't understand why until I realized there was a senator involved in the conspiracy. I didn't back down. And I ended up shot." She tapped her shoulder again.

With the memory, the fish tacos and salsa weren't sitting so easily in her stomach. She could almost smell the stench of engine oil and blood. Picking up her coffee cup, she took a hurried gulp, a cleansing breath, and then another bite of her food.

"I'm sorry. I didn't mean to bring up bad memories." Ryker reached out and put his hand on her knee. He opened his mouth to say something else, but his phone rang. He pulled it out of his pocket and sighed. "Speak of the devil, and he will call. Do you mind if I take this?"

Rebecca shook her head and waved him to go ahead.

Ryker stood and walked to the doorway just as Hoyt appeared.

"Excuse me, Hoyt." Ryker stepped through the opening and answered his call.

Hoyt looked so guilty.

Rebecca dropped her head. "Let me guess. Something came up, and someone needs me?"

"Bailey called. She's done with the autopsies and wants to know if you want the rundown."

She pushed the remaining food away. "I already lost my appetite. Might as well."

17

Rebecca stepped out of the bright sunshine and into the cool dimness of the hospital hallway. Her date with Ryker had come to an abrupt end as an emergency on the beach needed his immediate attention. At least this time, it wasn't her job that had split them up. Well, technically, his interruption came before hers.

As always, Bailey was waiting in the hallway, leaning against the wall with her arms crossed.

"Getting some fresh air?" Rebecca asked as she walked up to the M.E.

"Cooling down. The walls out here are nice and cool on my back. I've been working all day, trying to catch up. Got a full house in there." Bailey blew out a breath and pressed herself a bit harder against the wall. "My back is killing me."

"Do you want to relax a bit before we go and look at the gruesome remains again?" Rebecca made the offer, but honestly, she didn't want to wait any longer. While it was nice getting home before midnight the past couple of days, two families deserved answers.

"Nah. Honestly, I'm grateful not to be home. My husband has the day off and thought it was a good idea to take the kids down to the boardwalk early and get them some fair food. Apparently, they're so hyped up on sugar, they're bouncing off the walls. I rarely let them binge on sugar. I know what it does to the human body, and I don't want that to happen to my kids."

She shook out her hair, fanning herself.

"But their dad doesn't follow the same rules?"

Bailey rolled her eyes. "He's worse than the kids. When I allow it, he always goes too far. Which is why he's now required to take care of the kids after one of their binges."

Rebecca laughed out loud. "That sounds like a self-correcting problem."

"If that were true," she sighed and stood up straight, "it wouldn't happen so often. How about we get this going?"

"I'm ready when you are."

"You're going to need a full set of gear. Your two weren't my only wet guests."

"Bunny suits? Or something more than that?" Rebecca really hoped it wasn't a full hazmat suit. Those things were so difficult to navigate in.

"Bunny suits and slippers."

Rebecca waved that off. "Not a problem. I'm curious as to what you have for me. But that does explain why you were so hot. Should we get something cold to drink first?"

"I'm cool enough now. Good enough for another couple hours or so." Bailey flipped her hair one more time to cool off her neck and back. "Let's get suited up."

Inside the medical examiner's office, they stepped into the required personal protective equipment. Both women did so quickly and with the ease of experience. Afterward, they entered the examination room and pulled on their face shields and gloves. The suits protected their bodies. The gloves protected the evidence. And the shields kept anything from splattering on their faces.

It was always disturbing when an M.E. insisted on one when they weren't actively doing an autopsy. Rebecca looked around the sterile area. All the overhead extraction fans were going at full speed. In addition to that, drying fans, the kind used after a fire, were placed in three corners to circulate the air even more.

They weren't loud, but the constant droning was oppressive. The heat from the running motors also raised the temperature in the room. In short, the normally cool and dry autopsy suite was warm and slightly humid—not a good thing. Which also explained why there were only two bodies currently laid out. The rest were most likely in cold storage.

"As you probably already guessed, we have two males. Your Samuel Graves is here." She pointed to the table with the more intact corpse, the one with the complete skull. "Basically, none of the major organs were left. Or the soft tissues. From the bones, we can also tell he was in his mid-sixties, which matches the known age of the victim."

Rebecca hated to be right about Skipper, knowing how much he'd be missed.

The M.E. pointed to Graves's neck. "Here are the remnants of his neck tattoo. I already put the enlarged photos I took of it in the case file for you. And his dentals also matched."

"Thanks." Now they wouldn't have to get a DNA match with Skipper's brother.

Bailey stepped over to the other body. "This is the trickier one." She pointed to the destroyed vertebrae and then up to the cracked skull. "Surprisingly, this blunt force trauma to his head wasn't what did him in. He died from a broken neck. I've estimated his age to be early to mid-fifties. Also, his fingers were cut off antemortem."

Rebecca bent over to inspect the nubs left on the corpse. "These weren't from scavenging?"

"Some of the damage was caused by predation, but if you look closely at the remaining phalanges, you can see the bones were sliced clean. You're not going to get that with a bite."

"Any idea if it was for torture or to hide his identity?"

"Dealer's choice. I can tell you the fingers were not taken off one by one. I cannot tell you the why on that. If you look closely, you'll notice I don't have all the bone stubs either. They probably got carried off. If you find them on your beach, do let me know."

Rebecca bent over to examine the metacarpals and phalanges on their remaining John Doe. "Even if it was done to hide their identification, it was useless. After dumping them in the sea, fingers wouldn't last anyway. That could mean whoever did this isn't experienced enough to know that, or they were careful not to risk the chance they were found first. But that's not what happened with Graves, correct?"

Bailey tilted her head to the side and pursed her lips. "Correct. His fingers were eaten the old-fashioned way."

"So my bet is on torture."

"Could be." She picked up a clipboard and passed it over. "That blue plastic I found might be an answer to that. Or raise another question. Either way, it's disturbing."

"I don't like the sound of that." Rebecca read the report. "You found it on John Doe's shoulder and neck and in Skipper's teeth?"

The M.E. nodded in response.

Rebecca wrinkled her nose. "Does that mean Skipper was alive when he was wrapped up in the tarp?"

"And when he was dumped in the water. His lungs were likely among the first soft tissues to be consumed by predators, so I had nothing left to check for fluid. Without boring you with the process I went through, I found diatoms in his bones. Skipper drowned."

Rebecca looked at the wrist bones again. "And they both had their hands bound."

"So tightly it left marks on the bones. You can see marks here and here." Bailey pointed. "There are wear marks on the radius and scaphoid."

"Scaphoid?" Rebecca pointed to the bones in the wrist. "One of those?"

Bailey grabbed Rebecca's hand, turning it over to inspect her palm through the thin latex gloves. "What happened to you?"

"It's nothing."

"I'm a doctor and that's not nothing. Spill it, or I'll make you wait here until the temperature liquifies what little remains we have."

Rebecca sighed and explained the ladder versus hurricane injury. "The doc at our health center cleared me. Really. Now, tell me what you found on the scaphoid. I honestly have no idea what I'm looking at." There was no need for her to pretend to know something she didn't.

"That's why I get paid the big bucks." Bailey straightened her bunny suit. "I can also tell you that the blue plastic was definitely from a tarp, which explains how the bodies are in relatively good shape considering they were submerged for so long. The plastic helped keep the scavengers at bay. It didn't slow down the bloat or the smaller ones from eating the organs. The bigger bites most likely didn't happen until the tarp broke apart from being submerged in saltwater for an extended period."

"But if they had bloated, the bodies would have floated up."

"At that point, it would have been a race between the

intestinal flora eating the body from the inside out and the scavengers forming holes in the body that would release the gases." Bailey moved halfway down the table and gestured to the waists of each victim. "Which made me pay extra attention. To see who won, you know. But that's when I saw this. These other wear marks."

"Why is this skin a different color?" Rebecca held back her impulse to prod it.

"Because it was compressed. It's on both bodies. The tarp was wrapped tightly around them and sealed. So tight that the water couldn't reach the skin."

"If they were far enough out not to worry about the bodies being seen, whoever did this could have just dumped the bodies without bothering."

"If they knew what they were doing. Yes. A slice to the gut, dumped in the water uncovered, they would have been eaten pretty quickly."

It was starting to make sense. "Instead, our murderer overthought things, chopped off some fingers from one of the victims, and wrapped them both in a tarp."

Bailey shrugged. "It's curious as to why only one man lost his fingers, though."

Rebecca had been thinking the same thing. "It is. That John Doe could have been tortured, or he could have been important enough that his identity needed to be hidden. Burritos them in the tarp, like you would do if you were disposing of bodies on land. That's what I like about you, Bailey. You don't always give me answers, but you always help me ask the right questions."

Rebecca's phone rang. She reached for her pocket out of habit, but she couldn't get at it through the bunny suit.

"I don't have anything else to show you. The rest of it's in my report." Bailey motioned to the doors. "Shall we finish up in my office?"

"Happy to. I can see what you meant about the heat in these things." Rebecca's phone chimed again, this time indicating she had a text message.

She started heading for the exit, and Bailey followed.

"And you've only been in here for a few minutes."

They pulled off their masks, gloves, and booties, then stepped out. Bailey started stripping off her suit as soon as the door closed. She let it drape around her waist once her arms were out.

"I've got the report printed out in my office if you want to grab a physical copy. Once you get me something I can compare it to, I can identify our remaining John Doe. I already have the dentals pulled for him. He only had a few teeth remaining in his upper jaw, and what was there included a dental implant. I took impressions, but it might be a long shot without the full set of teeth."

Rebecca stripped her suit off and deposited it in the hazardous waste bin.

Now that she was unencumbered, she pulled the phone from her pocket.

"Speak of the devil…it's the state police. They were going to search through the missing persons list to find possible matches."

She read the messages and responded, telling Lettinger she would be there shortly.

While Rebecca could get some of her questions answered with a phone call, she knew she'd feel helpless sitting behind her desk with no leads to follow. Every thread in the case kept leading her back to Norfolk. The drive would give her time to process what they knew and formulate theories.

"I might have something for you sooner than expected."

18

The trip to the Norfolk state police office was uneventful. She was more relaxed by the time she pulled into the parking lot. Driving often did that for her.

"Afternoon, Sheriff. Lettinger is waiting for you in her office. Go on back." The front desk officer Rebecca had met last time waved her through and pushed a button. "Third office on the right."

She gave him a thankful wave and walked through to the back. The door she was directed to was ajar, but she rapped on it anyway. The force of her knock pushed it open.

Lettinger had her phone up to her ear and raised a finger, asking her to wait. She motioned to the chair across from her desk.

"The sheriff is here now. I'll let her know. Thanks." She hung up the phone as Rebecca sat down. "You got here quicker than I thought you would."

"I was already some of the way here. The M.E. on the mainland had set up a show-and-tell for me."

Lettinger laughed and tapped on her keyboard. "That's

interesting timing. I just sent her a possible match. Want to tell me what she had to show you?"

"John Doe, early to mid-fifties, was murdered. Broken neck. He also had his fingers chopped off and his skull bashed in. Skipper was alive when they were both wrapped in a tarp and dropped in the ocean."

"That makes it sound like the unidentified man was the main target." Lettinger continued tapping away at her keyboard.

"I think you're right. I haven't found anything that points to Skipper as someone who would have any enemies. Pirates are still an option, though. It could have been an opportunistic attack."

"As I told you, I went through the missing persons cases. With that age to narrow it down, I think I have a likely candidate. Let's see if the medical examiner agrees with me. One of the missing had some dental work done about six months ago, so if this is the same person, his records should make for a quick ID."

Rebecca waited as Lettinger worked on her computer, checking to see if Bailey had responded. She had left the woman busy at work in her office, so it was possible that the question about their mystery man was about to be answered.

Lettinger blew out a breath. "Luck is with us today. M.E. confirms it."

Rebecca sat up straighter. "All right, who is he?"

"Edmond Chase. Reported missing last week." Rhonda slid a folder over.

Rebecca snatched it up. "That's a big folder for a missing persons case."

"That's his rap sheet. He's pretty well-known around here."

"A few drunk-and-disorderly citations, aggravated

assault, assault, fraud, and…" Rebecca kept flipping. "That's an awful lot of minor offenses and tickets."

"Did I mention that he's pretty well-known around here? In fact, the whole Chase family is notorious in the Norfolk area. They also have numerous ties to local organized crime families."

"So the local police force let him know he was always being watched by slapping him with any infraction they could drum up."

"How does a man like that fit in with the man we understand Skipper to be?"

Rebecca raised an eyebrow and looked up from reading the reports. "You're asking me?"

"I'm asking you." Lettinger leaned back in her chair. "This is your case. And I'm betting that you know more about organized crime than I do. So you tell me. What use could a crime family have for a man like Skipper?"

Rebecca thought she knew the answer Lettinger was looking for but wanted more information before committing herself to any theory. "What can you tell me about the rest of the family?"

Lettinger slid her another folder. "Edmond is married to Wanda Chase, a Norfolk resident. They have three sons, Lewis, Oliver, and Dirk. It's not the happiest family life, as you would expect. Check out the name of the victim in the aggravated assault charge."

Rebecca shuffled through the papers to find the right one. "Lewis Chase. He attacked his son with a wooden chair over the Thanksgiving dinner table?"

"Edmond wanted canned cranberries. Lewis made fresh. That's all it took." Rhonda motioned to the folder. "I didn't include them, but the pictures make it even worse. The chair was only the last weapon he used. He started with the saucepot the cranberries were cooking in. Suffered first-degree burns to half his face. After that, Edmond moved on to a ceramic platter, a rolling pin, a spatula...." She twirled her hand in the air, indicating the list went on.

That poor kid.

"That must have been a fun court case, hauling all that evidence out."

"When the rest of the family got involved? Yeah, it made the news."

Rebecca made a mental note to search for that news coverage later. Right now, though, they had more important things to do. "Would you like me to go with you when you inform the family that his body was found?"

Lettinger waved that idea away. "I think you might have that backward. I'm just the forensic go-between at this point. This is your case. Your lead. You're the one who found the bodies, after all. I'm just helping out with the evidence. If that helps me close some missing persons cases, too, all the better. But everything else is up to you."

"You mind if I keep these?" Rebecca held up the two folders.

"I made copies for you. Those are all yours. They're also linked through the NCIC to help you sort it all out."

God, Rebecca loved this woman.

"Thanks. That makes it even easier."

"Did you want me to go with you to do the notification?"

Rebecca shook her head and stood. "I can take it from here. Thanks for all this. Maybe I can finally start making headway into solving this case now that I'm pointed in the right direction."

Lettinger stood as well.

Rebecca waved her down. "You don't have to walk me to the door."

"I'm not. I'm walking *me* to the door. I was supposed to have a half day today, so I'm calling it quits before anything

else pops up. I only stayed this long to get you this information." The agent paused and glanced at the clock as she
opened the door. "Unless you'd like to get a late lunch with
me? Not a working meal this time."

Wait. Is she asking me out?

Rhonda's smile widened, and Rebecca's brain raced to
keep up. She'd trained with and worked alongside numerous
outstanding agents in the FBI who happened to be
LGBTQIA plus. Some she'd been lucky enough to consider
friends. In all honesty, Rebecca was a little flattered. Here
was a woman who'd carved out a successful career in a male-
dominated profession, and she was interested in Rebecca?
Except Rebecca wanted Ryker, and she hoped he wanted her.

Or maybe she read the entire invitation wrong?

"Sorry, I have a lot to do before I make the drive back to
Shadow Island. Thanks for the invitation, though."

Lettinger shrugged as if it didn't matter and walked out
the door. "Okay, it was worth asking. I don't have a lot of
local friends. My hours always seem to get in the way. Maybe
I'll ask Harry. You met him. He's at the front desk. Meals
always taste better when you don't eat them alone."

Rebecca smiled. She knew precisely how Rhonda felt.
Maybe she'd been wrong about it being a date. If Rhonda just
wanted to be friends, that was more Rebecca's speed.

Things with Ryker were slow-going, but Rebecca thought
it would be worthwhile in the end. If they could get more
than an hour together at a time.

"Harry, I'm heading out. You want to get some *linner*?"
Lettinger pushed through the door into the lobby.

"Ah, your infamous lunch-dinner combo. Where're you
going? I'm in the mood for pizza."

Rhonda did a little fist pump. "Have you tried the pizzas
at Hell's Kitchen?"

"Jeez, you gotta get off Granby Street. There's more to

town than just the strip." Harry left the desk and followed them out. "How about *you* join *me* for linner, instead?"

"Sounds like a plan." Rhonda stuck out a hand. "Sheriff, call me if you need any more help."

"Will do." Rebecca nodded with a smile. "You all enjoy your pizza."

As the pair walked away, arguing over the best place to go, Rebecca pulled her phone out of her pocket, tucking the folders under her arm as she dialed Hoyt's direct line.

"Hey, Boss. You've been at the morgue a long time. Do I even want to know what you two have been up to?"

"You would *not* believe how fast a crab can eat a kidney when they're put in the same bag. We had to spend forever going through the bags. I had to use a slotted spoon to do it. And a sieve. But the good news is, I found enough to make she-crab soup tonight."

As Hoyt choked, Rebecca climbed into the Explorer and struggled not to laugh. When he started gagging, she couldn't hold back any longer.

"Oh. *Gah*. You were joking, right?"

She nearly fell over in her seat from laughing so hard while trying to punch the next address into her GPS.

"I *am* joking. I'm not even at the morgue."

"That's it. You're not allowed to hang out with Bailey anymore. You're picking up too many of her bad habits."

"Hey, you want me to fit in, don't you? Don't all sheriffs rib their senior deputies?" She transferred the call to the speakers.

"You've developed a mean streak, Boss."

"I'm sorry." The apology didn't sound sincere through her fading laughter. "I'm in Norfolk. The state police were able to find a match for the second body."

"Good to know you were working and not just goofing

off with corpses. Having the boss do that really hurts morale."

Rebecca checked the time on the dash before backing out of the parking spot. "Boss is working hard, as always. In fact, I'm heading to Edmond Chase's house to inform his next of kin that we've found his body."

"Edmond Chase? That's his name?"

"Yup. It should all be in the file online. Native to Norfolk. So while I'm here, I'm going to drive over and make the notification."

Hoyt groaned. "You better hope they aren't eating she-crab soup when you get there."

19

The home of Edmond Chase was on the far western side of Norfolk. Considering she was so close to the port, Rebecca decided to make a quick stop at the Backwater Marina. Now that she had both names and more questions, she hoped to get better answers this time.

A closed sign still hung on the door. She knocked anyway, hoping Andy Woodson would be inside working. Peering through the glass, she didn't see him in the lobby area, so she gave the door three hard knocks. After a few minutes and still no answer, she tried again.

There was no sign of movement in the shop. In fact, it looked like a good portion of the place had been packed away already. Boxes were stacked all over, not in any order, but scattered around every part of the building she could see.

Woodson was packing up and doing it quickly.

What's the rush?

She stepped back and looked around. That was when she noticed that the sign had also been taken down. Coastal Tours was out of business and soon would be gone.

Was it not possible for Woodson to keep the business

afloat on his own? She turned to walk back to the cruiser. Getting his home address would be easy enough.

"Sheriff West?"

Rebecca turned to face the voice. It was Andy Woodson. He was walking up the sidewalk with a fishing pole over one shoulder and a tackle box by his side.

Maybe he just retired?

"I was afraid I'd missed you. Are you coming back from fishing or just heading out?"

"Coming back. I needed to take a break and clear my mind." He set his tackle box down. "Fishing's always helped me calm down. Losing my business has been stressful, but I still have the ocean to get me through it all."

Rebecca smiled, watching the man closely. "That sounds like a great way of thinking. Can you not keep it running without Skipper?"

"I could struggle through, barely making ends meet, but his boat was the main draw here." He wiped his forehead with his sleeve. "And I'm just not interested in losing the money I've saved up to keep a failing business afloat."

His words reminded her to inquire about any insurance policies that might have been placed on Skipper. As a business partner, Woodson could have taken one out on him, which might have given him a reason to get rid of Skipper and cash in.

"I take it you're here with more questions? Anything I can do to help, I will."

"Have you ever heard of someone called Edmond Chase?"

No sign of recognition flickered over the man's face. He pulled a ring of keys from his pocket. "Edmond Chase? I can't say I know the man."

That was an evasion if she ever heard one. "That wasn't my question, Mr. Woodson."

"Well, as I said before, I'm not too involved in Skipper's

part of the business. I didn't interfere in his business, and he didn't interfere in mine."

"And exactly what sort of business was he into?"

He began picking through keys, clearly searching for the one that fit the front door. Was he stalling? "That I can't tell you. I mean, I know he chartered out his boat. But what he did on his boat, I wouldn't know, besides offer the services you see on the flyer."

"You seem to be evading the question about Edmond Chase. Could he have been Skipper's last reservation?"

Woodson stuck a key in the lock but didn't turn it. "I suppose he could have been. Maybe. I can't say for sure. I mean, anyone could have been."

His eyes were sliding around, checking every nook and cranny.

Is he scared?

Rebecca decided to let him go for now. She could always track him down later if she needed to. But first, she had to learn a little more about Edmond Chase and why his name made Woodson jumpy.

EDMOND CHASE'S house looked like any other on the block. A cape cod in a reasonably modern neighborhood. The driveway held two cars with a third parked along the curb.

From the road, Rebecca could see a volleyball net set up in the backyard. Two young men were playing a slow and friendly game. Not so much an actual match, but more like catch as they knocked the ball back and forth while chatting.

The two looked alike. Close enough to be brothers. Chase had three sons, so she could be looking at two of them. Their ages were most likely in the files, but she hadn't checked them before coming over. But with the victim being early fifties, late teens to late twenties seemed about right.

Of course the kids had to be here. Notifications were hard enough to do without the victim's children around. Especially considering this family and its ties to organized crime. There was no telling how any of them would react to the news. They might even rejoice at finding out. Or collapse. Or lash out. Or who knew...maybe they were behind their father's death.

Rebecca kept an eye toward the backyard as she walked up to the front door and rang the bell. No one answered. The sounds from the back continued. They hadn't heard her. She rang the doorbell again and followed it up with a hard knock. No sounds came from the house, and no one came to the door.

Maybe they were all in the back and couldn't hear her.

Letting the screen door close, she walked around the side of the house. Before she made it to the back, she ensured her badge was on display and in clear view.

The boys were still tossing the ball and talking. It sounded like they were comparing colleges. The younger one saw her first and caught the ball instead of hitting it over the net.

"What's up?"

The older one had his back to her and turned around when his brother pointed. He shifted his body to stand between her and his younger brother. While his move was defensive, it was also automatic and done without malice. "Can I help you?"

"I'm looking for Wanda Chase. Is this the right address?" It was always best to open a line of questions with one you knew would be an easy yes. It made the person you were questioning more open to talking. She continued to amble into the backyard to join them.

Both young men nodded, but the younger one turned his head away while the older one kept his gaze locked on her. "Mom! There's a cop here looking for you."

The back door, which she hadn't seen earlier, opened, and a woman poked her head out. "What was that?" She turned from her sons and stared at Rebecca. The photo in the folder must have been a few years old, but this was undoubtedly the same woman. Her eyes narrowed as they landed on Rebecca. "A cop?"

"Yes, ma'am." She held up her badge so the woman could see it from a distance. "I'm looking for Wanda Chase."

"That's me."

"Do you have a moment to talk?" She glanced at the two young men and back at Wanda.

The woman's face crumbled, then screwed up in a scowl. "This about Edmond?"

"Yes, ma'am. Maybe we should talk about this inside." She tilted her head to indicate Wanda's sons as her eye gesture clearly hadn't registered.

Their faces blanched as their eyes went wide. Again, the older one moved to protect his younger brother.

"Alone," Rebecca added.

"I knew this day would come." Mrs. Chase pushed the door wider. "His family ties made certain of it."

20

R ebecca took a seat at the kitchen table across from
   Mrs. Wanda Chase, watching the other woman stare
at a beer she'd pulled from the fridge. She hadn't taken a
drink or said a word.

Which was fine with Rebecca. Silence was often an inter-
rogator's best friend.

Not that this was an interrogation…at least, she didn't
think so. Still, in the early part of an investigation, family
members were always considered suspects.

Honestly, Rebecca hadn't yet connected all the dots in the
complicated relationships within this case. She hoped this
conversation would help in that regard.

After a solid minute of silence, Wanda lifted the beer.
While she took a long drink, Rebecca took the opportunity
to give the open-concept layout a surreptitious once-over. It
was as basic inside as on the outside. The beige couch was
overstuffed and part of a matching set with a loveseat and
recliner. A laminate coffee table was bare of any trinkets or
magazines. There were no bookcases, which meant no titles

to scan. A big-screen TV was mounted to a beige wall like a big, black eyesore.

Family photos were scattered minimally throughout the area, but most of them only showed candid pictures of the mother and her three sons. There was a single professional picture, a wedding photo of a much younger Wanda and Edmond. They were both smiling and looked fresh-faced and happy. Edmond's hair was a thick auburn in the photo.

The beer bottle hit the table with a clatter. "He's dead, isn't he?"

That was blunt. Rebecca would be equally so. "Yes. I'm sorry for your loss."

"I knew he was dead. He's never been gone this long. I knew he would never leave me. Not if he could make it home. I didn't want to tell the boys, but I think they knew too." She rolled the bottle in her hands. "Are you sure it's him? Don't I need to come down and identify his body or something?"

There was a tiny thread of hope in the woman's words, and an expression that Rebecca hated to crush.

She had no choice. "No, ma'am. We identified him by his dental records."

"Dental? Not fingerprints?" Wanda's hands shook, rattling her bottle against the table. "Was he badly damaged?"

"We believe his body was in the water for over two weeks." It was the softest way she could phrase it. She slid a business card over. "You can contact the M.E. to claim the remains once all the reports and examinations are finalized."

Wanda took the card, read it, and set it back on the table. "The only time he ever left was to help out his family."

The comment came out of left field, and Rebecca was interested to see where she was going with it. Clearly, there was a lot of history weighing on the woman.

"His family?" Rebecca prompted.

"I was never sure what they were into. Edmond refused to tell me. He had no contact with them when we got married. His family wasn't even invited to our wedding." Her gaze wandered over to their photo. "We were so young and hopeful. We talked all the time about our plans, our goals, and what we wanted to do in our lives. He always wanted a daughter. A little girl he could spoil rotten and treat like a princess." She smiled as tears finally trickled down her cheeks. "Instead, we had three boys. And he treated them like princes. He was always so proud of them."

Proud of them? And yet he put one of them in the hospital and went to jail for it over a difference of opinion on cranberries?

This was no time to argue, though. Rebecca was after information. "I'm sure he was."

"But then…" Wanda looked away, her gaze trailing to a different picture—one where she was holding a single child. "We got a call in the middle of the night about ten years ago. He said it was a family emergency and ran out of the house. It took a full day before he showed up, and the boys and I were so scared. We had a big fight, but he refused to tell me where he'd been. After that night, he would get phone calls at random and would just take off."

"Who do you believe the calls were from?"

Disgust flicked over Wanda's face. "His family."

"What do you think they wanted?"

Wanda shook her head. "I don't know, but he finally told me a few years later what happened on that first night. His father and brother were killed. And since then, he needed to help with the family business."

"What's the family business?" Rebecca asked softly.

"Nothing he wanted to talk about, but I heard rumors. People would whisper about us when we'd walk by downtown. Some restaurant owners would give us free food.

Edmond would come home with the most random things. Dirt bikes, jet skis, clothes, jewelry, new rims for our cars. It was all so arbitrary, but he said they were gifts from family and the friends of his family."

"You never asked who those people were?"

"Of course I did!" Wanda slammed her hand down on the table. She immediately looked contrite. "Sorry."

Rebecca understood the high emotion the woman must be feeling. "It's okay. What happened when you asked who those people were?"

She scrubbed her face with both hands, her pale skin reddening under the abuse. "He'd get angry. He always complained about his father's temper and said that was one of the reasons he and his dad stopped talking. I'd never seen Edmond's temper get out of hand until after his dad died. Over time, it got worse and worse. I tried to smooth everything over, protect the boys from his wrath. After a while, I just couldn't anymore. We had to learn to deal with it."

Rebecca couldn't stay quiet anymore. "Is that what happened on Thanksgiving? You just dealt with it?"

"That," Wanda jumped up and pointed a finger at Rebecca, "was an accident. That's all it was…an accident and a misunderstanding. And Lewis blew it all out of proportion. He refused to listen to his father. Even when Edmond tried to apologize."

Rebecca lifted an eyebrow. "Was he apologizing for the cranberries, the rolling pin, or the chair?"

"The cranberries! It was an accident. A simple cooking accident that happens in kitchens all the time. The handle of the pot was hanging off the stove. Edmond must have hit it. He talked with his hands a lot when he was angry. When Lewis got burned by the hot, syrupy sauce, he went crazy and attacked his father."

Had she heard that right?

"He…Lewis attacked Edmond. Your son attacked his father?"

Wanda sank down into her chair. "Maybe attacked is the wrong word. Like I said, it was a misunderstanding."

"Is Lewis here? Is he one of the young men outside?"

Wanda shook her head. "I haven't seen Lewis in…in a while." She sighed. "He took off a few months ago. He was sick of all the drama and the whispers and the stares. He moved to Colorado with some friends. That was before Edmond went missing. And he told us not to contact him again."

"Lewis chose not to have any contact with Edmond the same way Edmond had with his own father?"

What is this family into?

"Well, yes. But he didn't really mean it." A tear dripped off Wanda's chin. "He was just angry. You know how young men get. They have to defy their fathers and go out and live their own lives, so they feel like men. Edmond understood. He even invited Lewis down for a fishing trip a few weeks ago."

That was an intriguing bit of information. If Lewis left before Edmond's disappearance, and then they planned a trip together afterward, it would have been right around when Edmond went missing.

"A fishing trip? Where?"

"I'm not sure. There are so many fishing spots around town. Edmond used to take the boys fishing all the time. It was their father-son bonding time. He'd take them all, or if they needed special attention, he'd take them one on one too. But I think he wanted to make this trip special. Rent a boat and go out to Quell Island."

"Quail Island?"

"The little island," she said, as if Rebecca should know about it. "It was always a favorite spot of theirs. Edmond meant it as a way to mend fences after that unfortunate event. That was their special spot. I always thought it was just an excuse to be out in the sun, drinking beer." She picked up a paper napkin and began tearing it into shreds. "They'd always come home with coolers filled with empty bottles and little else."

"And he was planning to rent a boat for this trip?"

"I think so. He always did before. We didn't want the hassle and expense of owning a boat."

A rental boat out of Norfolk? And from a place he used often? Rebecca would need to ask Special Agent Lettinger to review Skipper's reservations further back than just June. Could that be what linked Edmond to Skipper?

"Did Lewis and Edmond go on that last fishing trip?"

Tears started to fall again. "No. Lewis called and left a message on the home machine, saying he'd changed his mind and canceled his part of the reservation. I'm sure it was because the move to Colorado was so recent. You know how hard it is to get into a new routine after a move." She shredded a long strip of napkin. "Ed was so mad about that. He was really looking forward to that fishing trip. He thought it would make things right with Lewis. He just wanted to have a good relationship with his oldest son again."

"What did Edmond do?"

"He...left. He said he was going fishing anyway. To clear his mind."

"Do you know who he rented the boat from?"

Wanda shook her head. "I don't know. That was the boys' thing. I didn't get involved. They just always said they were going out with the skipper."

"A skipper like a boat's captain? Or a man named Skipper?"

Wanda's brows came together in what appeared to be

genuine confusion. "I don't know. They just always called him a skipper."

"And what date was that trip planned for?"

"That's a date I'll never forget. It was the last day I saw my husband. June twelfth."

The same day Skipper went missing. There were too many coincidences. Lewis canceling, then Edmond still going out would explain why the reservation had been erased from the register.

"Have you heard from Lewis since then? Do you know if he went on that fishing trip after all?"

"No. I don't know. I haven't heard his voice since that message. I don't even have his new number, so I can't call him. I keep sending him emails, but he never responds."

Was that because he succeeded in cutting off his family? Or because he died on the boat with his father? Was there a third body out there yet to be discovered? Or had Lewis killed his father instead of accepting his apology?

21

I t was a beautiful, sunshiny day. The temperature was in the high seventies, with a steady sea breeze to keep things cool. For the third of July, it was a miracle that the weather was so perfect instead of blazing hot.

Rebecca sat in her new chair at work hunched over her desk, writing a report under the fluorescent lights. The clock on the wall ticked loudly. Normally, she wouldn't notice, but everyone was out taking care of other business. The empty building amplified the sound of the seconds slipping by.

A reminder that time was running out. That a killer was out there while his victims' remains had been scooped into bags. Friends and families were grieving. There couldn't even be a more traditional funeral with an open casket because—she shivered—that would be a horror show.

And that was why she was working in the office when she could have taken the day off, intent on transcribing her notes from the conversation with Wanda Chase. Now that she was, the fine details prickled at her.

Lewis had moved far away. He said he wanted no contact but then initially agreed to the fishing trip. Why? To make amends after distancing himself? Or to set his father up? Or something else?

Lewis agreed to the excursion, then canceled his part of the reservation himself. That meant he knew when and where his father had planned to go. Rebecca's intuition screamed it was too coincidental. Too neat and pat.

And where was Lewis?

A quick search hadn't turned up a new address for the young man. Unless the oldest Chase son was choosing to live off the grid in the Centennial State, her gut told her Lewis might not have moved at all. If he was choosing to live out of the reach of his father, Rebecca should still be able to find him with the resources she had at her disposal. Yet there was nothing.

So far, she didn't have enough evidence to obtain a warrant for his banking and credit card details. That information might just help them locate the wayward son.

That smudged line in the ledger kept sticking in her mind too. Was it just an error? Was it their reservation? Perhaps forensics would've figured it out by now. After she got this finished, she'd check to see if the report on that from the VSP had been added to the file yet.

Her direct phone line rang, and she picked it up. "Sheriff West, how can I help you?"

"Hey, Boss."

Please don't be another dead body. Please, please, please.

"What's up, Frost?" She forced a lightness into her tone that came off sarcastic. "Need help with traffic patrol?"

"You shouldn't sass someone who comes bearing gifts."

Rebecca blew out a relieved breath. "I hear cars and voices. Are you calling me from the middle of an intersection? Shouldn't you be focused on making sure our visitors this weekend don't clog the streets?" She ran a hand through her hair and tightened the thick ponytail at the base of her neck.

"Are you accusing me of being a slacker? I'm wounded."

"Uh-huh. Sorry. But why *are* you calling? And how do the streets look?"

"There's a lull, and I'm taking my contract-mandated fifteen. Doc says if I stand in one place for too long, I'll get sore."

"Is that why you sound winded?" She was immediately concerned but played it off. "Frost, are you doing yoga in the middle of Main Street?"

Hoyt chortled. "No, ma'am. Just some stretches to keep things loose. Anyway, a deputy has a lot of time to think when they're on traffic duty."

"And...did you solve our murders and end world hunger?"

Another laugh interrupted his panting. "That last one's above my pay grade. I'll leave that to you. Hey, you're wasting my break. I'm calling because I just remembered Angie asked me to call you yesterday."

"Oh?"

"She wanted me to let you know there's an event at Sand Dollar Beach today. It goes on all day, but we won't miss anything if we don't get there until after work. We'd like you to join us for the cleanup party."

"Cleanup party." Rebecca grimaced. "That sounds like an oxymoron."

"Nah, it's kind of fun. We started doing it a while back, mostly as a way to pre-party. Like going out the day before to set up a campsite. That's basically what this will end up being. You saw how we threw down at the post-funeral get-together for Wallace. It'll be like that, but with less crying and a lot more beer."

That didn't sound bad at all.

"Okay, I'll definitely consider it. Thanks for the invite."

"No sweat. Are there any new developments on the double homicide case?"

"I visited Wanda Chase's yesterday. Her eldest son, Lewis, cut off contact with his dad after Edmond went to jail for assaulting him. He moved to Colorado a few months back. Wanda believes Edmond was trying to make amends with his son, or at least win him over, and scheduled a boating trip for June twelfth. Lewis called and canceled his reservation, then informed his mother by leaving a message on his parents' landline. But Edmond took the trip anyway."

"And he went missing for two weeks before his body washed ashore. Is the son's lack of contact out of the ordinary?"

"No. In fact, Lewis Chase told his mother he was going to change his number. But I haven't found a new address for him. If he's living in Colorado or another state, I should be able to find at least a trace of him. Apartment rental. Job. Utilities. Even if he's subletting, there should still be a trail. And there's nothing. Not even on social media."

"Hmm, that is an issue." A horn blew in the distance and Hoyt yelled something she couldn't make out before returning to their conversation. "I can see that. We can do some further digging."

"Maybe. I only looked briefly. I was more focused on getting this report written and into the file so everyone would be in the loop on the latest developments."

"Sounds good. I need to get back to my corner. It's a beautiful day out here. Not gonna lie, I don't mind this task one bit."

She smiled. "Just remember that when the mainlanders get off work and start streaming across the bridge."

"Fu…crap. Thanks for the reminder. Maybe this Fourth won't be filled with idiots."

She forced a laugh. "Don't get your hopes up."

Hoyt ended the call, and Rebecca stared out her office door, hit by a wave of loneliness she couldn't explain. The absence of her parents was an ever-present ache, but as Independence Day grew closer, that feeling had intensified.

"Get over it."

Giving herself a mental shake, Rebecca reviewed her report. It was done, so she saved it, and added it to the file. There, she saw a new report from the Virginia State forensic group.

"Please tell me you found the killer's DNA and have already tossed him in jail."

No such luck. Instead, she was faced with a lot of technobabble that explained the process of how they'd recovered the erased portion of the log. She skimmed over that part and got to what she hoped would be the conclusion she'd been looking for.

It was.

Brent, the forensic tech in Norfolk, had retrieved the erased information and included an image. Edmond and Lewis Chase had been signed up for a day trip on June twelfth. Lewis's name had a line drawn through it, then the whole thing was erased. She reread the report, but there was no additional information. The writing matched the chicken scratch in the rest of the book, so it definitely belonged to Samuel Graves.

But there were no signatures or smears where the renter would have signed in and out for the reservation.

Edmond Chase had been on the boat, though. So why hadn't Skipper made him sign the log? Had it merely been an oversight? Or had the father and son fishing trip turned into something nefarious?

22

E ven a simple walk in the park was aggravating—really chapped my ass. I wanted to come out here to calm down and think things over. Staring at the ocean always did it for me, cleared my noggin. Nothing had been going as planned these last few weeks, and all I'd been doing was playing catch-up. I had to start thinking about the future.

But there were people everywhere, laughing, talking, playing games. Kids, dogs, more kids, with the usual suspects rolled in, pretending to be smooth criminals by hiding vodka in water bottles. Like anyone's fooled when they poured their "water" into soda cans and juice bottles. *I see you, dumbasses.*

And the idiots got even worse when they wandered. Which they did, on holidays. It was only half past noon and a quarter of them were already buzzing. Tomorrow, the Fourth, was gonna be the worst.

Independence Day used to be a good time. Something I could look forward to every year. There were family barbe-cues on the beach, sparklers for the kids, and noisemakers attached to bikes cruising up and down the streets. That was how we used to celebrate. Times were changing, though, and so was the island.

Now, every summer, the town was overrun by these idiots. The outsiders outnumbered the locals, and each tourist season was getting worse. Shops were full, restaurants had two-hour wait times, the beach was packed day and night, and even the parks didn't offer a hint of privacy or the quiet I sought.

You didn't have to be a damned Buddhist monk to need some peace and quiet. I kept moving. There had to be someplace left that the out-of-towners didn't know about where I could be alone to think.

I was walking because of traffic. On an island as small as this one, walking shouldn't have been an issue. But here I was, dodging squalling brats and inebriated parents and all the trash they'd left in their wake. The one upside of that was the adults never noticed when I shoved one of their spoiled crotch goblins out of the way. It was a fun way to pass the time.

Hearing them whine about skinned knees was a nice change to the screaming demands for ice cream or whatever they were begging for when I kneed the back of their legs. *Oops, sorry, li'l guy, my bad.* Back in my day, no one spoke to their parents like that. Mine would've beaten the shit out of me no matter where we were.

Then again, I learned early not to bother asking my parents for anything. I just took it instead. If they found out later, there would be hell to pay, but it was better than the alternative. I would rather die than whine and cry like that, even at that age.

When I rounded the turn that led up to the next beach, I paused. *What the fu—*

A crowd was gathered on the path, looking at something.

Now what? Why can't these assholes just go to Florida and keep the hell off Shadow Island? It's so hard to get any work done when there are people all over the place.

Whatever they were looking at couldn't be too interesting. People were still hanging out, leaning against trees, chatting, and sucking down drinks. Maybe it was some kind of show. But it was only the adults. The kids looked bored as hell and were poking around on their electronic devices on the outskirts of the mob. So it was nothing gruesome. The adults would have been agitated and the kids would have been enamored if that had been the case.

People I didn't recognize moved out of my way as I got closer, and I could finally see what they were looking at. Which was…basically nothing. A group of locals cleaning up debris. That was what had caught their attention?

Imbeciles.

One group was cutting the larger pieces of leftover wood into logs and stacking them for firewood next to a firepit with a metal ring around it. Another team was sorting the beached fragments between burnable, which was piled next to the wood, and nonburnable, which was being packed away in garbage bags.

Then I understood.

It was just a group of locals setting up some sort of campsite on the beach. Camp chairs, tables, and tents were waiting in a cleared area off to the side while they kept working.

Oh, this must be the site for the fireworks staging and the party for tomorrow.

I'd heard the fireworks were being moved to the beach the day before. That way, they could be quickly and easily loaded into the boats away from the docks and crowds. But first, the area had to be prepped and volunteers would camp here overnight to stand guard. This would happen when there was a chance of the weather not cooperating. This was what made this town so perfect.

Predictability.

They did this last year too. And the year before. They never changed. Just modified the way things were done when the weather forced them to. And that was the way I liked it.

That was why Shadow Island was the perfect place to hide in the shadows and move merchandise with no one ever noticing. Once I knew the routines of the islanders, the troublemakers were easy to avoid. Like beat cops who walked the same patrol every night on schedule, so you planned your break-ins for just after they passed this block or that shop. It was all a façade—local security—which made it even less secure because people thought they were safe.

And speaking of beat cops, I'd passed Deputy Frost back on Main Street as he attempted to keep the interlopers moving and not completely choke off the roadways. And Deputy Hudson was roaming through this crowd along the nearby boardwalk, looking more like a participant than a guard dog. Was he even working?

Oh, there he goes...

Sorting and bagging the trash while townsfolk set up tents next to a large pit being dug in the sand. That was where the whole pig was gonna be roasted overnight.

That pit was probably what had interested most of the crowd. It was a three-foot-deep, five-foot-long trench that, once finished, would then be lined with palm leaves and burlap.

I'd seen the same thing every year.

But never at Sand Dollar Beach.

They usually reserved this beach for the smaller, calmer, more sedate celebrations. Birthdays, graduations, wakes. I supposed they had to use it this time for the town-wide celebration because of the storm damage on the southern side of the island.

As if he could feel my eyes on him, Hudson glanced over. I had to fight not to freeze up or look away. I had to appear normal.

Hudson smiled as he recognized my face. I smiled back, lifting a hand in greeting.

He waved back.

People saw what they expected to see. So long as I kept acting like my normal, happy self, he would never suspect me of anything.

But if he ever did…

I slid my hand down, making sure my weapon was still safely hidden in the leg of my pants.

If Hudson or any of the pigs or anyone at all suspected me, I would take care of that problem the same way I'd taken care of the others.

While I was still debating all the ways I could eliminate him if necessary, someone called out to the deputy, and he turned away. I took that opportunity to leave. I had places to be and things to do. Work was just getting started, and I had to be ready for the festivities tomorrow.

So I could take advantage of the distractions.

23

A s Hoyt's radio crackled, he cursed under his breath. "What's happening now?"

A month ago, his balls hadn't shrunk into his body each time his radio jumped to life. But that was back in the days when there was so little crime on Shadow Island that having a mic connected to his shirt wasn't a necessity.

It was a necessity now.

Using one hand to direct oncoming traffic, he used the other to depress the button. "What's up?"

"Deputy Frost?" The voice didn't belong to Viviane, as he'd expected. In fact, it wasn't someone he recognized at all.

Then it clicked. The department had started using a new company for after-hours calls that went through an outside service. It was one of Rebecca's ideas on how to make things run smoother and give them some time off. But it wasn't after hours. Hoyt surmised that Viviane had stepped away from dispatch and had switched incoming calls over to the service.

"Yes. Deputy Frost speaking."

"We've received a 10-35 at Shadow Inn."

Hoyt had to rack his brain to remember what the code meant—domestic disturbance.

The department hadn't used proper codes in years. Looked like he'd need to brush up on the lingo with the new system in place.

Hoyt pinched the bridge of his nose. "I'm currently on traffic duty." Hell, he couldn't remember the code for that. He rushed on. "What are the details?"

From the corner of his eye, he spotted Greg Abner coming his way. Once again, the supposedly retired Abner had been pushed into service. He didn't seem to mind, and Hoyt wondered if Greg missed the job.

Hoyt mouthed the word "domestic" to the older man.

Greg rolled his eyes before waving for him to go. He knew Hoyt would rather do just about anything else, including possibly visiting the morgue on a hot day. Dealing with a domestic disturbance wasn't anyone's cup of tea.

And he'd be right.

DDs had the highest possibility of becoming weird very quickly, especially when it happened at a rental, like a hotel or an inn. Couples or even friends could get up to the strangest shenanigans when they were on vacation. Hopefully, they weren't drunk. Or stoned. And no kids or pets were involved. In any case, he would most likely have an amusing story to share later. As long as no one ended up hospitalized or dead.

"We currently have two separate calls of a man and woman arguing in their room but no room number," the dispatcher said. "The manager was informed of the disturbance by the guests. He also said he was going to go check it out. So keep an eye out for him."

Shadow Inn had been bought and sold recently, and Hoyt didn't know if the management had changed with it.

"Did you get the name of the manager?" It always sucked

showing up to a call without knowing who the victim or aggressor was in a case, and the manager could shed some light on that, hopefully. It was even worse when you showed up and there were three or more people and no easy way to tell who else might be involved.

"Ezra Pike said he'd be the one with the big ring of keys."

"Inform Mr. Pike I'm on Main Street and will be there shortly."

"10-4. Good luck."

It was a quick walk to where he had parked but an even quicker drive if he used the back roads the tourists weren't aware existed. As annoying as these types of calls were, he was thankful it wasn't anything crazier. Things had been way beyond the norm for too long now.

While he appreciated everything Rebecca had done for them, he was also relieved to know that this was something simple enough that he didn't need her help. Much like the D-and-D Darian had done the other night.

He hopped in his cruiser to go suss out the situation, hoping to diffuse things before they escalated too far. It wasn't a task he enjoyed, but it beat dealing with bloody anything any day.

Hoyt sighed, pulled out of the parking lot, and maneuvered to the closest back road. Despite Greg's efforts to provide Hoyt with a clean getaway, traffic was thick as people fought each other to make it to the beach and start their holiday picnic plans. By the time the real festivities started tomorrow, they'd all be sunburned and heat-exhausted.

Tomorrow, the crowds would start earlier, with the truly dedicated getting out to claim a spot on the beach bright and early. Which was when the walking hawkers would show up with their cold drinks and whirligigs to distract cranky children from parents who were starting to get overwhelmed.

He maneuvered through a sandy side road that ran parallel to the main drag, careful to watch for strays, or employees taking a break behind the various businesses. Just ahead of him on the left, he recognized the delivery area for Shadow Inn. He turned to park his cruiser directly in front of it, behind the building.

Before he even had time to shove the Explorer into park, a naked man stumbled out of the bushes right in front of him. The man was looking over his shoulder, his junk swinging for all to see.

"Oh, boy."

The streaker caught sight of the cruiser and froze as his eyes went wide with panic from either the deputy or because the road was scorching hot under his bare feet. Whatever the reason, he turned away from Hoyt and began to sprint, his white ass bouncing with every step.

Cars were forced to slam on their brakes to avoid hitting the man as he darted through the heavy traffic like an indecisive squirrel. Several more honked their horns, and a few people whistled and catcalled.

Hoyt's radio crackled to life. "Deputy Hoyt, the manager is still on the call and says the male in the domestic dispute has fled the room. He lost sight of him, but be advised, he's not wearing any clothes."

Hoyt glared at the device and snatched it up with one hand while flipping on his flashing lights with the other.

Greg's going to have a good laugh at this one. I hope the naked bastard isn't wearing sunscreen if I'm the one who has to catch him. Or tanning oil.

"Roger that, Dispatch. I've unfortunately got eyes on him now. All of him. Thanks for the heads-up."

With a string of curses, Hoyt flung open the door and took off running.

24

It had been a full morning of going over paperwork at her desk. Rebecca hadn't meant to spend so much time in the office today, not while her deputies were either out patrolling the beaches for drunks or pickpockets or standing on the hot pavement, directing traffic. She'd felt guilty sitting in the air-conditioning, and had finally forced herself out of the building a little after one.

Since this was her first holiday on the island, she was still learning the ropes.

Hoyt had mentioned there was a cleanup crew working on the site where the July Fourth party would be held at Sand Dollar Beach. The paid crews were setting up a pavilion on the sand, while citizens were setting up a camp in the park. It was a brilliant idea, to have a campsite near the beach so they could avoid the traffic tomorrow.

Rebecca was making her way there now, but it was slow going. For some reason, there was a traffic snarl in the other lane. As she inched closer, she could just barely make out flashing red-and-blue lights.

She frowned, stretching up in her seat to try and see over

the stalled traffic. People started yelling, and she rolled her window down to hear what was happening.

A skinny, pale, middle-aged, stark-naked man darted out from between two SUVs. He looked terrified as he sprinted in front of her cruiser. His hands slapped against her grill as he tried to sidestep around the big vehicle.

"Sorry!" He turned and kept running, cutting through a nearby gas station parking lot.

Rebecca swerved out of the lineup easy enough, pulled in behind him, and parked. As she jumped out of her vehicle, Hoyt ran past her, panting.

"You…gonna…help?"

She groaned. "This is what I get for complaining about paperwork." She took off after Hoyt and the naked man, who kept trying to look over his shoulder as he fled.

Seeing her joining the pursuit, he fueled his pace with a burst of speed and disappeared into a residential area.

Rebecca stretched her stride, catching up to her taller deputy.

"Go…right!" Hoyt veered to the left.

They split up, each running through yards and tiny gardens. A man with wide eyes and an unkempt beard turned, saw her, and then pointed to another yard to the left of where she'd been heading. Rebecca went where the civilian directed and prayed there were no kids outside playing.

She dodged a boat on a trailer in a cement driveway and saw a streak of white buttock as the man turned the corner.

He was trying to lose them by doubling back the way they'd just come. Or maybe he'd just realized he wasn't going to get far without any clothes on and was running back to get some.

"This is the sheriff!" she called out, happy that she still had air in her lungs. "Stop and drop to the ground."

The man glanced back again and stumbled over something she couldn't see. As his arms pinwheeled through the air, she closed the distance between them.

He was still scrambling to get his momentum back when Rebecca lunged forward. Her arms wrapped around his chest. As they fell, she worked to get a grip around him, her cheek sliding down his bare back, landing on his buttocks. She cursed as they hit the ground.

His breath whooshed out, and for a moment, he was stunned. Holding his cheek against the grass, she tucked a knee into his spine, immobilizing him even further.

"Do not resist!" She twisted his arms behind his back and leaned forward.

Even with all her body weight pressed down on him, he continued to struggle. "Get off me!" As he tried to wriggle his arms loose, she yanked them higher up his back, causing him to cry out in pain.

"Shadow Island Sheriff. Stop resisting."

To her surprise and relief, he went pliant under her knee. Rebecca took the moment of respite to wipe his sweat from her face with her shoulder.

"Aww, dammit," he cried out and began to sob. "She's gonna call my mom."

What the hell?

"Who's going to call your mom?"

"My wife."

Hoyt appeared at her side, cuffs in hand. He dropped down beside her and snapped the metal on the man's wrists.

"I think you've got a lot more to worry about than your wife calling your mother."

The streaker shook his head. "You've never met my mother. She's Catholic."

Rebecca shot Hoyt a questioning look, but he shook his head.

She pushed to her feet. "You take him. I've got a towel in the cruiser."

Though she still had no idea what was going on, she figured she could find out after she made sure he couldn't flash anyone else.

It was a quick jog to her vehicle and back. She heard the man complaining before she'd even made it back around to the side of the house.

"Come on, man. At least let me roll to my side. This grass is itchy."

"Then you shouldn't have gone for a naked run. What did you think would happen?" Hoyt glanced up as she came into view and rolled his eyes.

"I didn't think I was going to get tackled to the ground by some chick!"

"That chick is the sheriff. And that's what happens when you run from the police. We have to tackle your ass. Be glad it wasn't me, because I weigh a lot more than she does."

"She wasn't wearing a badge. I didn't know she was a cop."

The excuses were starting already.

"Actually, I am wearing a badge. And you could clearly see that I was in a sheriff's department vehicle."

He tried to crane his neck to see her.

Rebecca stepped around him. "You ready, Deputy?"

Hoyt nodded. "Let's get you up."

Working together, they lifted the man to his feet and Rebecca tried not to grin as Hoyt had to wrap the towel around the man's waist.

"Now, let's get you back to the inn and figure out what's going on."

As they hopped out of Rebecca's vehicle and strode over, their "streaker" in tow, his wife and the manager of the inn were waiting.

Rebecca left Hoyt to take the statements while she went around back to move and secure his cruiser for him.

The wife was crying and had her bags packed by the time Rebecca made it back.

That was when they finally got the whole story behind the domestic disturbance call.

Apparently, the wife had come back early from a walk on the beach and found him trying to seduce the cleaning lady without a stitch of clothing on. It wasn't the first time she'd caught him stepping out on their marriage. He tried to explain that he was drunk and thought the cleaning lady was her.

The wife didn't buy it, which started a fight that got loud enough the adjoining rooms called 911. By the time the manager showed up, the wife was launching shoes at her spouse like water balloons and said she was going to call her mother-in-law.

That had sent him running.

Since the wife didn't want to press charges, and the fight hadn't turned physical, he was arrested for public indecency and disturbing the peace. The wife had no plans for waiting around, though, and loaded up her car to leave. She was nice enough to leave her husband a change of clothes, so he didn't have to sit in jail naked.

Rebecca left Hoyt to finish it up and headed back to the station to start the paperwork. If they hurried, she might even get Coastal PD to give him a ride to the mainland so he could await his court date in the luxury of a real jail cell.

Getting arrested on a Friday sucked.

25

"Never a dull moment around here."

Rebecca looked up from her computer.

Hoyt was standing in the doorway, leaning against the frame like always.

"Did you get him booked?"

He nodded with a grin. "I even let him get dressed before I took his pictures. He's going to have a hell of a time explaining all this to his mother. Can you believe that guy is thirty-six?"

She laughed and shook her head. "And he's still afraid of his mom. I can't tell if that's a good or bad thing."

"Considering how much stupid shit he got up to just today, I'm betting on bad. Fear of her isn't helping him make wise decisions."

"Just makes him want to hide them more." She printed off the form she'd been working on. "Did he ask for a lawyer?"

"Nope. He just plunked down in the interrogation room and hid his face. I don't think he wants to talk to anyone." Hoyt watched her as she pulled the paper off the printer and read over it. "Is that your report?"

"Just for my side of the takedown. You need to write up yours still. But I did enter all the pertinent information for you, so it shouldn't take long. This is a pretty open-and-shut case."

Hoyt grinned. "Thanks, Boss. I'll get started on that right away."

"I'll call Abner and see if he wants to get some hours in today with babysitting duty. If you hurry, you can probably drop him off at the station and still enjoy some of the afternoon." She signed her report, put it in a file folder, and handed it to him.

"No can do. Abner relieved me on traffic control. He's there for another few hours."

Rebecca frowned and chewed on the inside of her lip. "I suppose I can sit here and—"

"And nothing. You go. This is my collar, so I have to be here. Besides, I need to get caught up on the murder cases. Unless you want to fill me in."

"Not a lot to fill in since we spoke earlier. We're waiting on additional forensics to come in. But we did get the report on the ledger."

"Did it confirm what you were thinking?"

"And everyone's stories so far too. The smudged line was the reservation Edmond had made for him and Lewis. Lewis's name was scratched off. Then the whole thing was erased. But Edmond still went out with Skipper that day and we don't know why."

"So it could have been a last-minute thing."

"Could be, but why erase the entry? My gut is saying it could've been something illegal since his son wasn't going to be there to see what he was doing."

"And Skipper was in on it?"

"Or got dragged into it, thinking he was helping someone out. Hard to tell. There's nothing else connecting the two men except that Skipper was the one who would captain the boat he rented to take his sons on fishing outings. Nothing points to Skipper being anything but a skipper, in fact. He did well with his business but didn't have an obscene amount of money in the bank. No deposits that wouldn't line up with his legal dealings."

"Wrong place at the wrong time, you think?"

"That's what it's looking like so far."

"But what do you think it was? You're the sheriff. What's your unofficial hunch?" Hoyt leaned back and looked up and down the empty halls. "No one's here but you and me, so spill."

"Spitballing ideas to see what sticks?" Rebecca rolled her theories around in her head.

"Sure." He finally moved to one of the guest chairs. "Why not?"

"I think being a well-known, family-oriented businessman would make a damn good cover for taking boat rides out to points unknown. I think he could have easily been catching more than just fish. I'd like to run the names on the ledger and see how many of them have rap sheets or ties to organized crime."

"That sounds like a good idea. And I bet that agent up in Norfolk wouldn't mind running those names either."

"Lettinger? Yeah. She seems extremely competent." Rebecca opened her email and composed a message. "What about you? You know more about fishermen and boating than I do. What do you think could have led to their deaths?"

"Edmond Chase was involved in organized crime?"

"His family was. He'd left the business. But from what I can piece together, he went back to it after his father and brother's death about ten years ago."

"What about the rest of his family? Not his wife and kids,

but other brothers, sisters, uncles, cousins, that kind of thing?"

"That's a good question. I haven't checked into all of them yet." Rebecca glanced up as she clicked send. "You've got a real mind for this."

Hoyt smiled but his eyes were sad. "Wallace and I used to sit around and bounce ideas back and forth like this. I learned almost everything I know from him. I really wish you'd been able to get to know him better."

Emotion burned Rebecca's sinuses as she thought of the late sheriff. He'd been a kind man, that seemed certain. Whether he was a *good* man was something she never got the chance to learn. "You're not the only one. I can't imagine how rough this has been for you."

He raised one eyebrow. "Learning how to work with a new boss?"

She shook her head and looked around the office she now occupied. "Coming in to work every day to see someone else sitting in your friend's chair."

"Ah, but you're not. You gave that seat to his brother…as a memento." Hoyt nodded to her new office chair.

She forced herself not to squirm. "His chair was too big for me anyway."

"I couldn't have sat in it either. The job's not for me. I'm a beat cop. This," he waved his hand back and forth between them, "I can do. But I can't put two and twoscore together as fast as you can."

Rebecca snickered. "That's forty-two."

He grinned, his eyes lively. "See, I didn't even know how many a score was. Chasing down domestics, dealing with drunks, having your back, I can do all that. Kicking the newbies into shape. Following up on leads you tell me about. This is my job. And I like to think I do it well. But the intuitive leaps you make, I could never do that."

"You just don't want to have to do all the paperwork."

Hoyt laughed. "There's that too. There's so much of it. I've got enough to deal with already. You can keep all that admin stuff for yourself."

"Well, I'm glad you're here. You can help kick my rookie sheriff butt into shape."

He bobbed his eyebrows. "I might even teach you how to drive a boat one day."

Rebecca held up a hand. "That you can keep. I've never been overly fond of boats."

They both grew somber, and she thought that he was thinking the same thing she was…

Or yachts.

26

Independence Day morning was turning out mighty fine, indeed. Hoyt grinned as he opened a box left by the delivery guys late last night to reveal the brand-new utility belt he'd ordered.

Viviane clapped her hands. "Oh, this is perfect. Rebecca's going to be so happy."

He held the belt up, inspecting every inch to make sure it was the right size. "Thanks for helping me pick it out."

"Of course. She needed something better than what she'd been using. No offense to Angie. The utility belt she threw together for Rebecca was so thoughtful, but—"

Hoyt held up a hand. She didn't need to explain. An officer's utility belt was an extension of their person, and an ill-fitting one was unacceptable.

Viviane clucked her tongue. "She's been so worried about getting stuff for us to make our jobs easier, she hasn't even thought of herself."

"You can say that again." Hoyt placed the belt back on the sheriff's desk.

They'd have to order Rebecca some official uniforms

soon. Not that her current "uniform" of khakis and polo shirts was bad, but their sheriff deserved to look like the person leading their little team.

Moving through the door of Rebecca's office, trailed by Viviane, Hoyt accidentally kicked the old broken plastic chair resting in the corner. He moved it farther out of the way and pointed to the broken slats on the back.

Viviane frowned. "How did she manage to do that? I never did ask."

"Pretty sure that one was my fault," Hoyt admitted, shamefaced. "I pissed her off, and she stood up too fast." He'd deserved the lecture she'd given and the strip of flesh she'd chewed off him that day. Since then, he'd been determined to do better and not follow the mistakes of Rebecca's predecessor. "The chair slammed into the wall and broke."

Viviane tapped her lower lip with a polished red, white, and blue nail. "Maybe we should get rid of that old thing and move her new chair and the desk farther away from the wall. Ya know, in case you do it again."

"I don't plan on screwing up that bad ever again." Regardless of his words, Hoyt went ahead and pushed the desk away from the wall just a few more inches. Things didn't always go as planned, after all.

After placing the broken chair in the hallway, Viviane returned with a red, white, and blue bow in hand. She tied it on the new belt, receiving an approving nod from her coconspirator.

With everything set up, Hoyt dropped down into one of the guest seats. "Yeah, this is so much better." He stretched his legs out and crossed his ankles.

"Don't get too comfortable. You've still got a partial shift today, right?"

He sighed and wrinkled his nose. "Yeah." Despite the

affirmation, he clasped his hands behind his head, savoring the surprise they had planned.

"When is Rebecca showing up?" Viviane slouched down in the chair next to him, so she could rest her head on the back of it and close her eyes.

"Hopefully not today. But you never know with her. She stayed here so we all could enjoy the pre-party."

They both groaned when Hoyt's phone rang. He pulled it from his pocket and gave a relieved sigh. "It's the other boss."

"Can't leave her hanging either." Viviane got up to give him some privacy.

He answered as she disappeared. "Hello, dear."

"Hey, hon, are you going to be coming down today?"

As always, when Hoyt heard his wife's voice, he smiled contentedly. "I hope to."

"But you don't have any active cases, do you?"

"We've still got those two dead guys to figure out."

He hated that this case was taking so long. Maybe he was just getting too used to how efficient his new boss was. If this had gone the way of the other cases, it would've been resolved already. Not that it was her fault, with the amount of evidence they had to go on.

Angie chuckled. "They were in the ocean for two weeks. I think that might be a cold case now."

Hoyt smiled. He could always trust his wife to make things seem clearer than he could see them. "Only temp-wise, dear. We still need to figure out who done it. There are some details that came to light yesterday that we need to follow up on."

"Well, fine. Do your job. I'm going to start in on the margaritas soon."

He glanced at his watch. Almost eleven thirty. "I do get a lunch break. How about I bring over some fish fillets? I know they're doing tacos at the stand, but the restaurant is still running, and they have a bigger selection and sides."

"That sounds like a good compromise. But I still expect you to try and be home for dinner. I didn't spend all night cooking just for you to skip out on it."

Hoyt hated to disappoint his wife, but with his job, he could never predict his schedule. "I'll try."

"Okay, fine." She huffed out a long sigh, but Hoyt knew she wasn't mad. "Do your best, and I'll see you if I see you."

"You're the best." He meant it. "You know that?"

"I know. Just make sure you never forget."

"Never."

Hoyt dropped the phone in his pocket and walked to the front door, shooting Viviane a little salute as he went past. "I'm heading out to lunch. Give me a call if Rebecca shows up. I want to see her face when she sees what we got her."

"Tell Angie I said hi, and I'll see her tonight."

"Will do."

The cruiser was parked at the curb for easy access. He hopped in and drove around the corner. Normally, he would have walked the short distance to the Seafood Shack, but he wanted to get the food to Angie as soon as possible.

When he got out, he spotted Ryker Sawyer standing in line.

"Hey, Hoyt, how goes it? Tackle any more streakers this weekend?"

Mike Smith, the owner of the establishment who was working the register, burst out laughing. "Streakers? Male or female?"

Hoyt grinned. "What do you think?" Then he turned to Ryker, who had no idea how badly he'd just set himself up. "That wasn't me yesterday. It was your girlfriend. You should have seen her wrapping her arms around that sweaty dude and slamming him to the ground like she was trying out as a lineman."

Ryker's jaw dropped. "You mean Rebecca did that?"

"Do you have any other girlfriends?" Mike reached out to punch Hoyt in the shoulder.

"Technically, I don't have a girlfriend at all…yet. But are you serious? Rebecca took him down?"

"She did. Ran right past me, looped around, tackled him, and had him pinned by the time I got to her." Hoyt just wished he'd had that body cam device Rebecca kept talking about getting them. He'd have watched that takedown over and over.

"Oh, I gotta meet this woman," Mike said. "I've heard a bit about her before but didn't know she's that cool."

"You think that's cool?" Hoyt was just getting started. "She took down two human traffickers, on her own, during an ambush, then went on to save three little girls by talking down the third trafficker, who was holding them hostage at gunpoint. After that, she got the young girls hot chocolate and colored with them until their parents got to the hospital, keeping them calm and happy."

"Dude!" Mike punched Ryker this time. "You gotta ask that woman out."

Ryker practically preened. "She asked me out, actually."

"Way to go, man." Hoyt clapped him on the shoulder. "That explains why she's been trying to get out early every day this week."

Ryker's head fell back, and he groaned. "Yeah. And I've been working overtime. But I did get to have lunch with her the other day."

Mike passed Ryker two bags of food and leaned over, bracing his forearms on the counter. "All that extra work is going to end after tomorrow, right?"

Ryker shrugged. "It should. But it's not like I have set

hours either. And neither does she. So things haven't progressed much."

"She's only been here a few weeks, right?" Mike asked.

"Yeah, about that." Hoyt nodded, counting back on his mental calendar. Time was a funny thing, zipping by and crawling at the same time.

Ryker hefted the bags. "I better go. Vale will have a coronary if the fireworks don't go off exactly as planned."

Hoyt suppressed the need to curse at the sound of the man's name. "And I better hurry and get my wife's lunch."

Ryker laughed. "Better not let Angie get hangry."

Hoyt grabbed his arm. "Ya know, Rebecca'll be at Sand Dollar Beach tonight. You going to be there too?"

Did Ryker actually blush?

"I'll do my best."

Feeling as if he'd just made the world a better place, Hoyt placed his to-go order. He couldn't wait to tell Angie about the conversation he'd just had. He glanced over at Ryker just as he handed the bag of food he'd purchased to the ever-scruffy Mac, who was waiting on a nearby bench.

Ryker was a good man. He deserved to be with a woman like Rebecca.

27

R ebecca walked into the office just after four, not intending to stay long. She wanted to check up on the BOLO she'd set up for Lewis Chase and see if Hoyt had any updates on tracking down the rest of Edmond Chase's family.

Viviane popped up in her seat as soon as she walked in. Her normally bright smile had reached epic proportions. But there was a nervousness behind the cheer that Rebecca couldn't quite place.

Rebecca examined her closely. "You okay? Lines staying quiet?"

"Yup, surprisingly calm so far. Darian and Locke are working the beaches, and the staties are assisting. No big calls so far. Hey, uhm…" Viviane shifted from one foot to the other.

Her friend was acting awfully strange.

"Are you okay?"

"Yes! Can you get me a cup of coffee, please? I don't want to leave the phone if I don't have to. We're getting closer to fireworks time, and you never know what's going to blow up then."

"Um, sure." Rebecca walked over to the coffee maker and poured a cup, picking up two packs of sugar and creamer to go with it.

She carried it over and found Viviane tapping away on her cell.

"Here ya go. Is Hoyt back yet?"

"Thanks." Viviane set down her phone and took the coffee. "He's just around the corner."

"Fantastic." Rebecca turned toward her office. "Tell him to come find me when—"

"What happened with the naked dude?"

Rebecca glanced at her watch. "He should be settling into his cell at Coastal right about now. Didn't you see Coast PD come get him?"

Viviane waved a hand. "I know where he is. I want to know the story of how you caught him."

Why was Viviane acting so strange?

She faced her friend. "Are you okay?"

Viviane's head bobbed up and down. "Of course. I've heard rumors going around, but I want to hear the real story from you. So I can set people straight on it."

Viviane was clearly hiding something, but Rebecca decided to humor her a bit. "Not a big story to tell. I was driving out to Sand Dollar…"

As Rebecca retold the story, Viviane reacted with exaggerated expressions that became more curious by the second.

"I wish I could have witnessed that." Viviane fake-gagged. "Except for the sweat to the face. That's pretty gross."

Rebecca's cheek tingled from where she'd scrubbed half the skin off. "It's part of the job."

For the first time since she'd walked in, Viviane's expression softened. "You love what you do, don't you?"

Rebecca didn't hesitate. "I really do. I love taking care of people and keeping communities safe."

Pressing her lips together, Viviane opened a drawer, pulling out a book. *Criminology for Dummies.*

"Viviane, you're no dummy." She reached over and took her friend's hand. "You know that, right?"

Viviane lifted a shoulder. "I know. I just thought it was a good place to start."

"Start? Viviane, are you interested in becoming a deputy?"

Viviane flipped through the book, keeping her eyes down. "I am. Is that stupid?"

Rebecca's heart broke a little at the question, and it took everything inside her not to pull Viviane into her arms. This was a professional question, and she needed to keep it on that level.

"It's not stupid at all. What you currently do in dispatch is already an important role, and you do that beautifully. I see no reason why Shadow Island, or any community in the world, wouldn't be grateful to have you on their law enforcement team."

The corners of Viviane's mouth tipped up, revealing a tiny bit of that beautiful smile. "I signed up for classes because I've been inspired by watching you."

Emotion rushed to Rebecca's face, burning her sinuses. She blinked to keep it away. "You'll be an asset to the profession. If you ever have questions or—"

"Questions about what?" Hoyt asked as he came through the door.

Viviane shook her head, a clear signal that she wasn't ready to share her desire to follow in Rebecca's footsteps just yet.

Rebecca winked at her. "Questions about how to take down a streaker. I was thinking about hosting a class next weekend."

Hoyt laughed. "Well, you're certainly the expert on that." He shared a look with Viviane that Rebecca couldn't quite read, then turned back to her. "Hey, Boss, did I tell you what happened when his mother arrived as we parked outside the mainland department?"

"Nope, but I can't wait to hear the story."

Hoyt turned away. "Let's go to your office and I'll tell you everything."

Viviane unplugged her headset. "I want to hear too."

Rebecca was confused. "Why can't you tell us here?"

He just kept walking. A second later, Viviane followed.

Not sure what was happening, but game to find out, Rebecca followed them to her office.

She saw it right away. How could she not?

The black, nylon duty belt was perched in the center of her desk with a small patriotic bow resting on top.

Viviane giggled. "It was Hoyt's idea. I just helped him pick it out, make sure it was the right size." Viviane scooted into the corner of the small office. "Do you like it?"

Rebecca wasn't sure how she felt. She actually really liked the cobbled-together duty belt Hoyt's wife had made for her. But at the same time, it was a bit big and heavy, and didn't provide room for all the various holsters she preferred to carry. It didn't distribute the weight of her tools correctly, either, which was something she'd been noticing more and more. The leather caused her to sweat more too.

This one, though…

It was perfect.

She touched the one at her waist. "Won't Angie be upset?"

Hoyt snorted. "That thing was always meant to be temporary. This one is official. And it'll do everything a good duty belt should."

Rebecca was touched, not only by the gift, but also by the excitement Hoyt and Viviane were clearly feeling about presenting it to her. She wandered behind the desk and ran her hands over the various holsters and pouches.

She removed her current belt and set it on the desk. Untying the bow from the gift, she unbuckled the belt and slipped it around her waist. After ensuring it was the right size, she took it back off and began positioning her weapons and tools.

Rebecca fought back tears as she avoided the expectant gazes of her coworkers. Her friends.

"I think she likes it," Viviane whispered loudly.

"She likes it very much," Rebecca said, with a smile that lit up her whole face. She put the heavy belt back on and adjusted the pouches until the weight was correct. "Yeehaw, partner."

"And now we're in the Old West. Maybe we should have bought a pink one to knock you down a notch." Hoyt laughed and held up his phone. "Smile for Angie."

Rebecca struck a pose, her thumb tucked into the belt.

"Seriously, you two, thank you so much. This is amazing."

"It wasn't just the two of us. We took up a collection, so Vale couldn't find a way to block it."

Rebecca smiled at their deception. "So everyone was in on it?"

"Yup. It's from all of us." There was a flicker in Viviane's eyes that let her know not everyone had given, or at least not given evenly. "Getting you properly uniformed is next."

Rebecca grinned down at her khakis. "I'm not proper now, huh?"

Viviane waved a hand. "You know what I mean." She headed for the door. "I'm going back up front."

"Thank you, Viviane." Emotion threatened to choke Rebecca again.

Viviane winked. "You're welcome. Now, you and your new belt go solve this double homicide."

"Will do." Rebecca sat down behind her desk, amazed at how comfortable the belt was. She'd need to fiddle with the pouches and holster placements later, but she was thrilled with the gift.

Hoyt cleared his throat. "I know you're enamored with your new toy, but I'm thinking we better talk about the case."

She eyed the space around her. "Did you move my desk?"

He chuckled. "You don't miss much, do you?" He tapped his knuckles on the wood. "Case? Remember?"

Rebecca forced her fingers away from the double hand-cuff pouch she'd been adjusting. "Right." Focusing, she recounted their status. "We've got BOLOs out for the boat, the son, and the rest of the family, and I'm waiting on warrants for all the financials I can get my hands on. Other than that, I have nothing. We don't have a location or even a weapon. Not even a good motive."

"My fishing buddies didn't notice any strange boats around, so there goes the pirates idea. But I was reading up on the case earlier today. Didn't you say the wife knew where they went fishing?"

"Yeah, Quail Island." Rebecca pulled up the case file. "But there's nothing like that around Norfolk. I even looked up fishing spots or bays that might have that name or—"

Hoyt was shaking his head.

"What?"

"It's not near Norfolk, but there's a Little Quell, Q-U-E-L-L, Island about an hour away by boat."

She grimaced. "There's not a handy bridge to the island by chance?"

He snickered. "Nope."

She glanced at her watch. "Won't Angie be expecting you at the beach?"

"She's already started drinking margaritas with her friends. And we had lunch earlier. Besides, we'll be back before dark and the fireworks. Come on. Time for a fun, new experience."

Rebecca grumbled and got out of her chair, dropping her chin down so he couldn't see her smile.

"Better not get my new belt wet."

28

H oyt stood at the helm, navigating the speedboat they'd borrowed through the open ocean to Little Quell Island. The boat belonged to a friend who never had a problem letting the sheriff's department use it, so long as they refilled the tank. It wasn't incredibly fast, but it was smooth enough, and got them where they needed to go every time.

Still, at the speed they were going, and with the choppiness of the water—thanks to all the other boats going around the island—the ride had been rough from the start. And yet, Rebecca didn't look in the least bit bothered, like Hoyt thought she would be. In fact, she looked bored.

He was starting to think he'd fallen for one of her tricks again.

Leaning against the side of the boat, her elbow hanging over the side, she stifled a yawn and stretched out one leg, her foot wiggling back and forth. Before they'd left, she'd had the forethought to grab her waders and put them on. The black rubber was still new and shiny.

Hoyt couldn't take it anymore and finally broke. "I thought you said you weren't fond of boating."

"I'm not. I always end up with hair plastered to my forehead and everything goes by so fast I can't enjoy it." Rebecca's voice sounded as bored as she looked, and she didn't even bother to look over her shoulder to talk to him. Fortunately, the wind blew her words backward.

He rolled his eyes. Then what she had said to him earlier hadn't quite been a lie. Though it had been incredibly misleading. He had to keep reminding himself that she was an excellent liar, even if she couldn't seem to keep the emotion off her face.

"But the upside is, we'll get there soon, right?"

"Yeah, it's right there." He pointed to a small island swathed in green that showed only thin strips of sand along its edges.

Rebecca lifted the dark glasses covering her eyes. "That barely looks large enough to be called an island. Does anyone live there?"

He shook his head and steered the boat wide to come in at an angle to the nearest strip of sand. "Not a soul. No electricity or clean water, so there are no houses or campsites. They keep trying to turn it into a nature preserve or wildlife sanctuary. So far, it hasn't stuck."

"Why not?" Rebecca shifted to her knees, the rubber squeaking on her legs, and leaned forward to take hold of the rope hanging from the cleat.

"Mostly because it's so small and insignificant, and because it sits in a way that the current washes all kinds of trash onto its beach. And when we get the big storms, anything that's put there as a marker or sign would just be washed away. There's no realistic way to keep it protected."

"That makes sense. It's so tiny."

"I'm going to take the boat as close as I can, but it looks

like most of the trees got blown over during the hurricane. Maybe we can tie off to a rock or something."

Rebecca stood but kept one hand on the rail. "It looks like it got squashed."

The trees weren't the only things that had been flattened. Grasses and flowers were laid out in a wavy pattern that showed the flattening had been done by the ocean, not the wind. Seaweed was woven through the plants. Stingrays, fish, jellyfish, and even seagulls were mixed into the rot as well. The smell was awful, even with the breeze blowing most of it away from the boat.

"Keep an eye on the prow and make sure I don't run into anything. This is going to get tricky." Hoyt shifted the boat left and right as he navigated through the water.

She walked forward and called out directions as he inched them along, helping him find a safe path to the beach in a surf filled with debris. Once he was close enough, Rebecca jumped down, holding the dock line she'd unraveled. The water was only up to her knees, well below the tops of her waders.

With the rope over her shoulder, she tilted her body forward, careful to use her arms more than her raw palms, and she hauled the boat in as Hoyt killed the engine. She didn't need to pull it ashore, so it was easy enough to lead the boat in. Once it was close enough, she tied the line off to the base of a cracked tree.

Hoyt jumped out once the boat was secured, barely getting his feet wet before trotting to the dry sand.

"Let's go for a stroll and see if we can find any evidence here." Hoyt looked up and down the barely visible land. "I don't think we'll have a lot of luck."

"Eh, it'll be a walk on the beach."

Hoyt groaned and started walking. "I knew I should have traded shifts with Darian today."

"That wouldn't have worked. He doesn't do sand. Remember?" Rebecca started shifting things out of her way, checking under fallen trees and grasses.

"He told you?" Hoyt stepped around a heavy branch.

She shrugged, bending over to shift a mat of grass out of her way. There was nothing underneath it but ripped-up soil. "Yup. He told me about the code phrase you used to get him to fix my truck."

He dropped his head and rubbed his neck. "I wasn't exactly subtle, I guess."

"Don't worry. I'm fine with him knowing about my little problem. And about him having his own triggers to avoid. Everyone has their quirks and issues."

She frowned and wrinkled her nose. Stirring up the island was a stinky, gloppy mess. Trying to move the flotsam out of the way just broke and slid it apart. Straightening, she used her rubber-clad foot to kick through the mess instead.

"We've got plenty of those here. This place is a bigger mess than the inside of my head. I can barely find enough ground to walk on and the foliage is too slick. I'm not sure how we're going to find evidence here. Anything like prints or drag marks is already gone. If there was anything to begin with, it's most likely buried in this slime."

Hoyt grunted as he slid back into the water. His waders were older and worn in, so they moved easily around his ankles as he got his balance back. "Or washed away."

"Let's make a full loop. We're here. It shouldn't take us long." Rebecca gestured to the small area there was to cover. "We can't cut through the middle anyway. And we're both dressed for wading."

Hoyt nodded, and they made their way around, having to move inland in some spots and out into the water in others. The beach was shallow, so that part wasn't much of an issue.

As long as they didn't go out too far, they could stay safely on that shelf.

"This is such a cozy island with a perfect beach for docking. It's a shame it isn't used more."

Hoyt held out his hands and gestured around them. "But there's no place to lie down and sunbathe or picnic. The trees aren't thick enough for good shade. Fishing is spotty around here too."

"That's too bad." Rebecca cocked her head. "Spotty? The fishing?"

A thought had occurred to Hoyt that he was going to keep to himself, as it might or might not be relevant, and if it wasn't, just saying the words could take Rebecca down a rabbit hole. But with her mind already reeling…

Hell with it. He'd tell her and let her decide what to do with the information.

"Something you'll find interesting is that I've heard the Yacht Club sometimes comes to this beach. It's more rumor than fact, but I thought you ought to know."

That got Rebecca's attention. "Why would they do that?"

"No clue. There's nothing on this island to protect, as I said. So we never looked into it. Most likely, they just use it as a waypoint. A meetup place before they go out to sea. There are a lot of places like that people use."

"But when you take into consideration that one of the people on the boat was in a crime family, the Yacht Club connection makes a lot more sense. We'll need to see if we can find other connections than just this place."

Hoyt ducked under a thatch of thick grasses held up by a twisted myrtle tree. "Do you think the two could be connected? The Chase family and the club? They're not rich enough to get a membership at the marina. Hell, they don't even own their own boat. That's why they rented from Skipper, right?"

Rebecca nodded. "As far as we can tell. But if the fishing is so spotty in this area, why did Edmond Chase come out here to go fishing?"

"That's a damn good point." Hoyt frowned and rubbed his bottom lip, then jerked and spit, as if he'd tasted something awful. "As if this case wasn't bothersome enough."

"There are all those records Wallace put together. We can go through those." Rebecca washed her palms off in the surf.

Hoyt winced, wishing he'd thought to bring an antibacterial rinse for her hands. "That would be our best bet."

The two worked in silence for a while. Hoyt stepped over a downed tree and almost fell on his ass. After catching his balance, he bent to examine the slick spot his shoe had landed on.

I'll be damned.

"Rebecca." He waved to get her attention. "Come get a look at this."

She squelched her way over. "What'd you find?"

He lifted a layer of soaked thatch. "I think this is decking. It looks pretty fresh to me." He bent over and started digging along the ground.

She began taking pictures with her phone camera. "How fresh? Are we talking last couple of days fresh, or last couple of weeks?"

With the hurricane, any number of boats could have been wrecked from anywhere along the eastern coast.

"Hell if I know. But it hasn't been here for years. Let's keep looking. Keep an eye out for anything shiny. Also, bits of brass, rope, painted wood."

Rebecca rolled her eyes. "Aye aye, Captain."

He grinned. "What color was the trim on Skipper's boat?"

Rebecca wiped her hands on her waders and pulled out her phone. After a few seconds, she held it out for Hoyt to see. "Red. That should help."

Hoyt looked around at all the detritus. "Maybe."

He wasn't certain how long they'd been searching before Rebecca grabbed something and pulled. "I found rigging." Shuffling forward, she kept lifting. The thick rope ended within four feet and flopped into her hands. It had been ripped apart.

"That wasn't exactly helpful." The *thunk* of wood on wood reached Hoyt's ears. "What was that?"

She crouched. "Holy shit."

When she stretched for another something, he headed her way. "Mind your hands. Let me."

She stood and pulled out her phone, taking more pictures.

Hoyt bent at the knees and hauled up a piece of the stern, knocking it against tree trunks as he pulled it free. The white wood really showcased the bright red paint that spelled out *um Runner* with *Norfolk, VA* underneath it.

"Skipper's boat was the *Chum Runner*." Rebecca took more pictures.

"Against all odds, I think we found it…or at least a part of it." Hoyt pointed at his feet. "I've seen enough hurricane damage in my day to say this boat was probably intact before Boris blew through. The raw wood edges are too fresh."

Looking down, Rebecca swept the ground free of the pulped plants and exposed the shipwreck they'd been walking on.

"Time to call in the big guns. We're way out of our jurisdiction."

Hoyt set down the piece he was holding and nodded. "Good, because I don't think we have an evidence bag big enough to hold all this."

29

R ebecca looked over her shoulder to see Hoyt smile as he started the boat and headed back to Shadow Island. They'd called in the Coast Guard. Only a federal agency had jurisdiction over an island that small. Several of their boats circled around Little Quell Island now.

And with the Feds involved, things could move more quickly. They'd already unearthed enough to be sure that it was indeed the *Chum Runner* that was wrecked against the shore. Now all she and Hoyt could do was wait while the techs compiled evidence for them.

Teams were working to haul up the pieces of the boat while divers swam around to check for any additional bodies. It was possible that Samuel Graves and Edmond Chase had been dumped in the ocean only a few nautical miles from the island. The swirling currents of the hurricane could have spun them around to land on the other side of the island from where they had started.

Hopefully, there wouldn't be any more victims. Two were more than enough. Though she'd love to know if Lewis had ended up being on the water with his father that day.

Hoyt was captaining the boat, so Rebecca could just sit and think. Which she'd done for the better part of an hour.

The dock was bustling. Even though they were still a ways out, she could see that. The sun was setting, so they were mostly just silhouettes swarming up and down. The boardwalk was also full of people as they got late dinners, played games, or shopped for souvenirs. Most of them, however, were heading out to watch the evening's annual show.

Fireworks over the water were a beautiful sight. But it was even more breathtaking from the water. The flutter and pop of the displays would dance overhead, as if the viewer were inside a kaleidoscope.

Or so she'd heard. Personally, she thought that was a bit too much. It was almost a waste. No one could look in every direction at once. She decided, though, having never experienced this kaleidoscope effect, she preferred sitting in a comfortable chair on the beach with the entire display in front of her where she could appreciate it, instead of breaking her neck to view it all.

But still, people were lining up to get on the boats. Beauty was in the eye of the beholder, after all. There was every kind of water vessel you could think of. Even some kayaks were heading out. The waters were filled with ferries, pontoons, party boats, yachts, and even dinghies by those who had staked out an early vantage point.

Hoyt had to thread a way through them all. A young man was waiting for them on the dock and waved to catch their attention.

"Toss him the rope." Hoyt pointed to him. "He probably wants to take over as soon as possible, so he can make some money taking a group out."

"Of course." Once they were close enough, Rebecca tossed the line.

The kid wrapped it so fast around the dock cleat, she couldn't even follow the loops. A noise from behind made her turn, and she saw Hoyt was doing the same. Just that fast, the ride was over, and the boat was secured.

"The sooner you help them off, the sooner we can get loaded up and on our way."

She didn't see who had spoken, but suddenly several people were reaching out to give her a hand up and out of the boat. Knowing she was holding up the line, Rebecca clutched an outstretched forearm to avoid damaging her palms and jumped out.

"You want to just send us the bill for the gas today, Silas?" Hoyt asked, shaking the hand of the young man she'd tossed the rope to. He couldn't have been more than twenty.

Impressive to own a boat at that age. She'd thought he was just helping.

"Sounds good." Silas clapped him on the shoulder. "And save me a serving of the pork, would ya?"

"You got it!" Hoyt stepped out of the way as a group of tourists started loading their things into the boat.

With that taken care of, Rebecca made her way through the press of people. Hoyt caught up with her when she hit the boardwalk. The crowds were a bit thinner here. People were still distracted by everything the shops had to offer and weren't trying to get anywhere, since the fireworks were still a little over an hour away.

Hawkers patrolled up and down as well, calling out their wares, tempting people with their pretzels, cold water, and glowstick wands. There was a festive feel to the air, the kind found at any fair across the country. Kids were laughing. People were playing games. And the smell of cotton candy was everywhere.

She took a moment to stop and smell the cooked sugar.

This was more like the Shadow Island of her memories. Full of life, laughter, adventure, and a cooling ocean breeze.

"We've got nothing else to do tonight. Do you want to just head back to Sand Dollar Beach and join the real party? We have backup from the mainland, remember? We can take the night off."

Rebecca looked around at the small campfires that spotted the beach, each swarming with people like moths to a porch light. Happy families gathered together for an extended weekend. Friends huddled up, laughing. Children running around forming new friendships. Some that would last for years, others for only a few hours.

She tilted her head up to smile at her deputy. "It is a holiday. And past our quitting time. We don't even have reports to fill out, since the Coast Guard is taking care of all that. You're right. That's why I requested extra backup. We all deserve a little break. Right?"

"Yup." Hoyt grinned.

"Then let's get moving." She motioned for him to hurry up and join her as she strode down the walk.

"We can even pretend to be vigilant and walk up the beach. You know, like we're doing a patrol of the partiers."

Rebecca stepped off the dock and down into the sand, looking for the quickest route to get where they were going. "Or we could just walk along, making our presence known. While we're heading for the drinks we know are waiting for us."

Hoyt chuckled and followed after her. True to his word, he kept his eyes roving, looking for any signs of trouble. "It's good to remember we're more than just the job."

"Oh, yeah, it is." Rebecca pulled the badge from her belt and slid it into her pocket. He might be willing to keep up the patrol, but she was totally checked out. Already, she'd put in more than enough hours this week. It had been the easiest one she'd worked here, but emotionally, it had been draining.

She'd ultimately failed to have dinner with Ryker this whole week because of the job. To be fair, it was due to both the hurricane and their careers. During the two breaks she'd had, she managed to squeeze in a quick lunch with Ryker and an evening chat with Kelly Hunt. The rest of her time was spent catching up on sleep. But every time her head hit the pillow, she'd dreamed of her parents.

While they'd been soothing, waking up had been heart-wrenching. And every morning was a reminder of just how alone she really was. The house echoed with it. The office nearly vibrated with it. Everyone else had been busy making plans and hanging out. She'd simply been going through the motions while trying to keep a smile on her face.

Tonight, before the dreams came back to haunt her, she was going to do her best to live in the present.

"Angie's going to be so happy. I told her I'd try to make it tonight. But she's going to be downright delighted when she sees you." Despite his words, Hoyt was still looking left and right, checking on the partiers to make sure everything was as joyful and harmless as it sounded.

Looking around now, things didn't seem all that fun and cheerful to Rebecca anymore. Everything was loud and full of movement. Hectic, chaotic, discordant even. Shaking her head, she tried to look at the partying again without the negative emotions tainting everything she saw. It was no use.

She kept expecting to feel something. The excitement she'd felt when she'd roamed these beaches as a child and teen. Or maybe even the joy she used to feel while at a beach party. But all those times before, she'd always ended the night…

Back where her parents were waiting for her.

They would sit on the beach together as the sun went

down. Right up until the fireworks started, they would chat about anything that came up. Nothing was out of bounds. It was on those nights that they truly bonded. Without them, with no late-night chats, tonight would just be lights in the sky in interesting shapes and colors.

She was afraid they would only be as captivating as the people in their brightly colored swimwear, with and without sunburns, dancing and frolicking around them. Which was to say, not at all. Turning her eyes away, she focused on the park they were approaching.

Still, it would be nice to sit back and relax with friends, even if they weren't family. To get to put her feet up and forget about having to be in charge. The last time she'd joined them for a picnic on the beach, it hadn't lasted long. But up until she'd gotten called away, the company had felt nice, at least.

Together, she and Hoyt stepped into the trees, avoiding the paths the tourists knew about, and walked directly toward the gathering. The ruckus of the parties behind them faded away. For a few minutes, they walked in peaceful silence.

It wasn't long before the lights were visible through the trees ahead of them.

Darian's laughter drifted over first. His face was lit up where he stood next to the small bonfire at the clearing. His feet were firmly on grass, not the sand he hated so much.

Rebecca grinned. Moving as quietly as she could, she stepped out of the trees behind him. "I thought you were supposed to be on duty, Deputy Hudson."

The people on either side of him fell quiet, and a few jumped as they turned to look at her.

Darian looked over his shoulder and laughed, not bothered by her fake scowl in the least. "Yes, sir. And the vigilant deputy I am, I heard a commotion over here and came to check it out. Turned out to be a beautiful woman dancing with an adorable baby." He had one arm wrapped around the shoulders of his wife, Lilian, while the other held their baby girl, Mallory. "I'll get right back to it now that I know everything here is all legal and peaceful, Boss."

Rebecca laughed and pointed to the empty place on her new belt where her badge no longer was. "Don't 'Boss' me. I'm done for the night. I'm just here for the drinks and food. And to give you a bit of a hard time."

"Yes, sir. I see you got your present. You like it?"

"She does, indeed." Frost stepped into the light of the fire.

"I'm glad. Hey, maybe I should stay here and make sure this one doesn't cause a disturbance for just a few more minutes." Darian grinned and bounced his daughter in his arms. The tiny girl gurgled, clutching at his uniform with her chubby baby hands.

Unable to help herself, Rebecca wiggled her fingers at the baby. She was just too adorable, the way she turned her badass daddy into a cooing mess.

"There you are, hon. I was wondering if you and Hoyt were going to be out on that boat all night." Angie walked over, a red cup in each hand, a slight slur on her tongue. She offered the full one to Rebecca. "You've never had my margaritas. Try one!"

Kelly Hunt laughed. "Or two!"

"Shift's over! Time to enjoy ourselves." Hoyt stepped around Rebecca and took the full drink instead.

Rebecca tried to put on a happy smile, but it felt too weak to maintain. Was tonight the night she'd get that margarita to sip on the beach while surrounded by friends? Or better yet, a beer? She'd take either.

"How about you?"

A hand brushed her arm, and she turned to face the voice. The smile that had been wobbling strengthened considerably. Ryker held out a beer that was already open. "Are you finally off work?"

"As of a few minutes ago," she assured him, taking the bottle and clinking it against his. "How about you?"

"Off the clock 'til morning." Ryker's eyes held hers as he took a deep pull. "I also brought a spare chair, if you want to join me."

"I'd love to."

"Keep your eyes on the sky, folks! The show is about to start."

Excitement bubbled up in Rebecca's veins as she followed Ryker to a pair of chairs. The canvas of the seat was nice and cool on her back. She slid back in it, stretching her legs out in front of her.

"Hey, Sheriff, you want a plate of roasted pork and potatoes?"

Looking around, she couldn't tell who had asked that, but Ryker tapped her hand and pointed to a man standing next to a table.

"I would love that."

"Coming right up!"

"And please, call me Rebecca when I'm not at work."

"Will do, Rebecca. My name's Logan Ashford." He walked over and handed her the plate.

The smell of roasted meat and potatoes made her stomach growl, and she realized she hadn't eaten since breakfast.

She narrowed her eyes at him. "Are you the *pool table dancing* Logan?"

The man reddened. "One and the same. Sorry about that."

She shook her head and picked up a potato with her fingers.

"Jeez, Logan. We are civilized around here," Angie teased, handing Rebecca a set of utensils wrapped in a napkin.

"Eat up, Rebecca. That's my special recipe." Hoyt gave her a proud nod over his red cup.

Rebecca took a bite and the meat melted on her tongue. "Oh, that's good."

There was a loud pop, and everyone stopped talking to look up. Despite sitting among the trees, the view of the fireworks was unobstructed.

Red, white, and blue lights exploded and sparkled down the night sky.

She set down her plate.

Ryker's hand slid over and wrapped around her fingers.

She held his hand and watched the horizon light up as the next barrage started. Looking around, Rebecca took stock of all the people with her. In the fading lights of the explosion, she could see there were many more people there than she'd noticed when she approached Darian at the fire.

Hoyt was standing with Angie. Darian was still hanging on Lilian while she held the baby up to see the show. Greg was back by the tables, pouring himself a drink. Viviane was also there with her mother, Meg. The younger woman caught her looking and winked, then looked pointedly at Ryker by her side.

Now this feels like home.

Everyone was so caught up in their own little celebrations and weren't paying any attention to me. Just the way I liked it. Twilight was nearly over. Only hints of light still remained in the sky. The fireworks were going to start at any moment.

I bobbed along, pretending to be staggering drunk and caught up in the music. Just another spectator, moving through the parking lot to get closer to the beach so I could see the show.

Tailgate parties had cropped up everywhere there was space to park a vehicle with a clear view of the sky. They didn't even need tailgates. Some of the parties were people sitting in camp chairs around the open trunks of cars. Which meant that the beach was probably shoulder to shoulder, and best avoided.

By moving from party to party, no one would remember my face tomorrow, if they even noticed I'd briefly been in their orbits. Hiding in plain view was a talent of mine and one I'd sharpened over the years.

Even with the contacts I'd groomed, I still preferred to

stay in the shadows. Especially when the Yacht Club bastards were being so uncooperative. If I ended up doing everything on my own, I could reap a higher profit, but the chances I would fail were higher too.

That wasn't going to stop me. Nothing would.

I danced and staggered my way across the beach. Blending in silently, belting out lyrics to songs, or calling for the fireworks to get started already. I was a chameleon, changing to fit the environment I walked through.

Once I hit the shadows of the woods, I could finally give up the act.

Picking up my pace, I walked through the park. I knew these paths like the back of my hand. It was easy enough to thread my way through the growth of trees between the paths and the beach, sticking to the brush as the light faded from the sky.

The boom of the first fireworks being shot off echoed up from the beach. In the flash of light, sprinkling down from the sky, I saw movement in the tall grasses and froze. I kept my eyes on the shadow as it shifted closer. All I could make out was the shape of a man mixed among the other shadows. I leaned back against the closest tree, hiding in the darkness of its leaves.

Whoever it was hadn't noticed me, as he kept moving along slowly. His head swung back and forth, as if searching for something. It was hard to make out any features until a sudden burst of white fireworks shimmered down, lighting up the wooded area again.

I knew those features. That prominent brow stood out easily. Squinting, I leaned forward. I recognized that face, even behind the shaggy beard.

Of course it had to be him. Because nothing could ever go to plan anymore.

"What are you doing here?" I kept my voice low so he wouldn't know where I was hiding.

He faded into the shadows again, half hidden by the night as the fireworks died out. He turned back and forth, looking over each shoulder as he tried to figure out where my voice was coming from. I wasn't surprised. He never did have a knack for this kind of thing.

"I'm looking for you."

He sounded so sure of himself. Certain in a way that only the truly ignorant were. "Why?" I made sure to put an extra bit of mockery in my voice just to piss him off.

It worked perfectly. Both his hands clenched into fists. Oh yeah, he wanted to beat my brains in.

"Because I want answers."

I laughed harshly. The boy was a regular comedian. Of course he wanted answers, but that didn't explain why he was looking for *me*. Or how he knew where to look. What brought him to this spot on this night?

"You're not going to find any answers here that you like. You should forget it. Go back to your life. While you still have one."

Never one to take good advice when he heard it, the kid finally figured out where I was standing and fumbled his way over. I wasn't trying to hide any longer. I'd wasted enough time.

"Is that a threat? Do you think I'm afraid of you?"

"Of course not. Why would you be afraid of me?" I snorted as he continued to stumble around even as the fireworks show peppered the landscape with bright flashes of light. "You're like your father, too damn stupid to be properly afraid of me. Because you don't know what I'm capable of."

"Oh, I know." His gaze finally landed on me, and I saw him clench his fists again. This time it was on purpose, not just a reflexive response. "I know what you did! I saw you get on that boat. You killed him."

When the idiot lunged at me, I started to sidestep but not quick enough. The kid was younger and faster. His shoulder caught me in the side, and he wrapped his arms around my waist, knocking me on my ass.

I didn't try to fight him. He had speed, but I had experience and no compunction. Instead, I rolled with his momentum, ducking my head into my forearm as his fingers came up to claw at my face.

The kid wasn't playing around. He was out for blood. It nearly made me laugh.

Turning into the roll, I flipped us onto our sides. I nearly got on top of him in that first clash. Before I could, he threw an elbow up and hit me in the jaw. That rocked my head back, but I didn't let go.

His fingers stopped going for my eyes and tried to wrap around my throat instead. This punk really thought he could kill me. How that would get him answers, I didn't know. It didn't matter.

I shrugged hard, tucking my shoulders up tight to my neck so he couldn't get a good grip. He didn't have the advantage of height or weight, but he did have youth and a shitload of adrenaline pulsing through his body. I struggled to push myself up, kicking my feet in the sand to gain purchase and finish rolling over.

He gasped as I pressed my hands against his neck.

Choking someone was a dirty, loud, slow business. It was also incredibly personal. Faces close as I watched the life fade away, holding their still bodies after they passed out but weren't dead yet. It took too long, way more time than I could afford, especially with the holiday, as anyone could walk up and see what was happening.

I didn't want the risk. It was a struggle as he kept fighting against me, but I managed to pull my knees under my body so I could press forward, pushing him into the sand and choking off his blood supply. This way was much faster. His muscles started weakening almost immediately.

But there was still a better way. I reached out with one hand while holding him down with the other. The kid was making gagging and choking noises. They weren't loud, but any noise was too much.

The backs of my fingers brushed against something hard and heavy. I wrapped my hand around it and got a feel for the heft.

Perfect.

I picked up the rock and smashed it down into his face as he stared at me. His nose exploded. I grunted at the mess but did it again. He fought harder as my hand slipped slightly. I put more effort into the strikes, pummeling his face.

It cracked, popped, and split, splattering dark blood all over. So long as he fought me, I hit him with the rock, in his face, his neck, his head. Anything I could reach.

Slowly, his hands lost their hold and slipped off my shirt. They fell like deadweights at his sides.

"Damn fool boy, how else did you think the night would turn out after you did something so stupid?" It should have been a shame, to kill someone so young and immature. But he'd brought this on himself.

A quick look showed there was no one else around. No witnesses, no worries. I shook the blood from my hands and felt a surge of warmth as I realized I had won. Again.

Except now I had a mess on my hands. I had to get this all cleaned up and the body moved and set in such a way that it couldn't be linked back to me.

I knew exactly what I needed to do. And now was the perfect time to do it, as the fireworks show was holding everyone else's attention.

31

The fireworks were long over, and most of the crowds had left for the night. There were only a few small gatherings left. Their campfires spotted the sand sporadically on the horizon. The sparks that swirled around them were like fireflies dancing in the breeze.

It was the perfect night for a walk on the beach.

"You know, strangely enough, now that we've actually got some alone time, I can't think of a single thing to talk about." Ryker rubbed his neck.

"Let's blame the beer." Rebecca waggled her bottle at him. This was her third, and it was half empty. She wasn't sure if it was the alcohol or the embarrassment of being in the same predicament as him, but her cheeks grew hot. "But we can talk about anything you want. As long as it's not about work."

"Definitely not about work." He shook his head. "How are things at the house? Anything come up that I need to fix?"

Rebecca snorted. "You've probably spent more time there than I have. Awake, at least." *That was such a lame thing to say.* As the handyman her landlady had employed, Ryker had gone over frequently but always while she was at work. That thought embarrassed her. She was sure he hadn't done anything like go through her drawers. Her esoteric books and DVD collection were a different story.

"I could ask about all those crazy cryptid documentaries you collect." It was like he was reading her mind. "Except it seems pretty obvious why you'd be interested in that."

Stepping around a tree, she kept her face away from him. "Because of the mermaid I met when I was a little girl on these beaches?"

Ryker ducked under a low-hanging branch. "You what?"

She burst out laughing and took another drink. "I suppose it could have been a siren, though. I'm never really sure what the difference is. Or I could be pulling your chain."

They passed through the last of the trees, and something on the beach caught Rebecca's attention as Ryker started chuckling.

"I was going to say it's because you're always looking for answers to unsolved riddles. And that probably had something to do with why you wanted to become law enforcement in the first place." Ryker looked over and saw her staring gape-mouthed at the ocean. "No, you're not going to fool me again. There's no mermaid out there. I've lived here my whole life, and…."

Rebecca pointed, distracting him. Surely, she had to be seeing things. With the back of her hand, she rubbed her eyes. This had to be a stress-induced hallucination. Or a nightmare. Their romantic moonlit stroll could not end like this.

"Not in the ocean. On the beach. Is that what I think it is?"

"What *what* is?" Ryker squinted in the direction she was pointing. "That's just someone passed out after too much partying."

"Not spread like that, it isn't." She could make out the

head, shoulders, torso, but with the legs splayed behind the body unnaturally like that, she knew. Even passed out drunk, no one with blood still flowing through their veins could lie like that. Or stay so still.

She dropped her beer and ran to the discarded lump on the sand.

"Rebecca? What the hell?" Ryker ran after her.

"Stay back!" The shape became more evident the closer she got. It was a man. His face was smashed in, and he had a blood-soaked shirt. "Call 911 and tell them to send an ambulance, and that police are on the scene."

"Let me help you—"

"Keep back. Don't contaminate the crime scene any more than I've just done."

A second later, Rebecca was happy to hear that he was doing exactly what she'd asked. Then she realized she hadn't asked but had ordered him. She'd have to apologize later.

Right now, she only had attention for the body in front of her. Out of habit, she pulled her flashlight from her new duty belt and swept the sand, looking for evidence and ensuring she wasn't disturbing the scene as she crept closer.

There was nothing. The blood on the man's face sat there, no longer flowing because there was no heart beating to push it out. He was dead.

Blood on the tiles.

Rebecca shook her head to remove the image of the dead girl from her mind. The first dead person she'd ever seen and the real reason she had gone into law enforcement.

Focus on the here and now. I really wish I hadn't had that third beer.

She squatted, taking in everything around her. Adrenaline mixed with training, raising her situational awareness. There were plenty of marks, but it looked like someone had raked a palm branch over the sand to hide their tracks.

That was not a good sign. It was what someone might do for a body dump.

Once she got a thorough look at the pulverized face with its ragged bits of beard mixed in, she knew there was no hope. No one could survive that. Still, she reached out and pressed her fingers against his carotid.

Nothing, just like she'd expected. Except…

He's still warm!

Rebecca stared down at the corpse and saw he was missing all his fingers and the thumb on his left hand.

Shit. Shit. Shit.

Her hand jerked to her hip without thinking. Her fingers wrapped around the butt of her gun, and she leaned over to check the right hand. It, too, was missing all the digits. Staying low, she shifted around on the balls of her feet, making herself as small a target as possible. Her eyes scanned everything.

She lifted her left hand to press her phone against her ear, speed dialing a number. Was the killer still out there? Was he watching them right now?

Did the shadows watch her every move?

Darian answered his phone with a laugh. "What's up, Rebecca? Did you get lost? Or maybe you need some advice on—"

"No joke this time." She kept her voice soft so she couldn't be overheard.

Ryker glanced over at her, and she motioned for him to get down. He dropped into a crouch.

"I need you to grab whoever's sober and meet me just north of the campsite. We've got a fresh body, and I need backup ASAP."

All the laughter disappeared from Darian's tone as it became coldly professional. "Yes, sir. How fresh? Who is it?" She heard voices calling out to him with questions as he moved through the crowd of people.

"He's still warm. I need you to fan out. We've got a killer loose on a beach full of sleepy, drunk tourists. As for who it is, I haven't the slightest idea. But I know we found the body before he wanted us to, so hurry."

REBECCA RELAXED a bit when Darian and Hoyt arrived at a dead run, stopping far enough back not to contaminate the scene.

Darian remained on the nearby grass, the way his body leaned betraying the war between his desire to get close enough to help and his need to stay off the sand. Making his choice, he raised his voice to be heard from his position. "We've got more guys coming."

Hoyt approached, moving Ryker back and out of sight of the corpse. Rebecca only had eyes for the area around them and trusted her deputies to keep the civilian out of the way.

"We'll wait 'til they get here, then." The buzz from her beers was washed away by anxiety and adrenaline. "Call the state police and ask them to reach out to Agent Lettinger in Norfolk. And ask them to please hurry."

"Yessir." Darian picked up his radio and sent out the call.

A few minutes later, Greg showed up with three volunteers carrying some of the high-powered flashlights they stored in the cruisers. She waved them over and directed each of them where to stand.

They didn't get close enough to the body to compromise the scene, only close enough that she could keep an eye on them. With the lights arranged to overlap, they could illuminate the landscape fifty yards in every direction.

The deputies moved out as soon as they had lights, guns

held at low ready. Rebecca watched their backs, the civilians, and kept her eyes roving, searching for the killer.

"Is everyone else still at the camp?" She spoke over her shoulder and saw two of the men jump slightly at the sudden noise. Until then, they'd all been speaking in whispers.

"Yup. I told everyone to stay together and in the camp area until we called to tell them it's clear." Greg was holding his light still, but his eyes kept moving, same as hers. "By the way, I'm not armed. I left it at home because I was going to be drinking."

His warning was clear. "That's always a good plan. For both of those. What's Locke's ETA?"

"Thirty."

"Don't worry, Sheriff. We got your back."

Rebecca saw the man who spoke for the first time in the light and realized it was Logan Ashford. He was still wearing the apron someone had draped over his neck back at the party.

"And we didn't tell people any gruesome details. Just that you needed lights, and everyone was to stay put until told otherwise. I reckon with that many people together, not even a psycho is going to try to attack there."

She didn't think they were in danger at the moment. After all, the killer could have used a gun with all the fireworks going off but chose a blunt object instead. That could mean he didn't have a firearm on him. A small relief. She wouldn't bet her paycheck on it, though.

"And people are still out on the beach. Or stumbling around." Logan's voice was grim, and his light wavered as he started to turn to look up the shoreline.

"Sheriff, we need more people."

"I know that, Greg. As soon as we're cleared here, I'll call in the cavalry."

A shadow moved on her left, and she swung to face it, raising the barrel of her gun slightly.

Darian flicked his flashlight up twice to signal her before he stepped out from behind a tree. "We traced the tracks and found the original crime scene and the murder weapon. It was a rock."

She nodded. "Where's Hoyt?"

"He's still back there." Darian nodded back in the direction he'd come. "I'm going to wait with him. We don't have a lot of light there."

"Greg, go with them. Three men can keep watch better than two."

"On it. Y'all listen to West here. She knows what she's about."

"I ain't moving a foot unless she tells me." Logan tried to laugh, but it was shaky.

Ryker clasped his shoulder, giving the young man support.

Bright light from the ocean washed over them. Rebecca's skin prickled with fear. All the civilians were between her and that light.

"U.S. Coast Guard, identify yourselves."

Rebecca didn't turn to face them so she wouldn't be blinded but lifted her badge over her head. She recognized that voice from Little Quell Island and let out the breath she'd been holding.

"Sheriff West and my deputies with civilian volunteers."

"Just the lady we were looking for. We heard you needed some backup and lights, ma'am. And since we were right around the corner, we decided it would be the neighborly thing to come over and help."

"Well, I asked for the cavalry, but Coast Guard is even better." Rebecca laughed, and the tension rolled off her shoulders as she turned and looked at the monster of a boat bobbing on the waves. The CG didn't have any real authority over this. But with giant searchlights bathing the shore and parts of the park, armed men in uniforms lining the deck, and a small boat coming to shore with more supplies and assistance, she no longer had to worry about how she could keep everyone safe. Two U.S. CG boats were more than she could have hoped for.

Darian gave her a sour look, knowing she'd managed to slight him in jest once again. "First the Marine Corps and now the Coast Guard? You really got no taste, Boss."

"Hey, when you're on an island…"

"Army boy is just mad he's outnumbered again." Greg laughed. "Guys, since Rebecca has backup here, how about we go help Hoyt and Darian get some lights set up at the other scene? Thank you so much for your help tonight. I owe you all a round or two at the bar."

"I'll be picking up that tab, Greg. Sorry your holiday was ruined." Rebecca turned around and saw how many people had been willing to drop everything to help her.

"It's about time you Coasties did something useful," Darian grumbled, loud enough for them to hear.

"Did you say something?" the officer asked. "I hear whining. I don't speak Army."

Darian laughed. "You protect us from fish. Do they give you guns or harpoons?"

32

R ebecca was standing next to the cruiser Locke had arrived in, as Agent Rhonda Lettinger approached. "Happy Fourth."

Lettinger shook her head. "You've become quite the magnet for trouble."

"I've noticed. But I'm just going to blame the currents. It makes it easier to sleep at night." She joked, but she knew this one would haunt her dreams for a while.

The faceless, fingerless man seemed so young. If they had worked faster or put more hours in, could she have prevented this death?

"There's nothing more we could have done."

She looked over at Rhonda, not surprised she had guessed what Rebecca was feeling. It was a common regret on a case.

Lettinger examined the scene as the techs swarmed. Like ants, they trailed back and forth, going over every blade of grass and grain of sand and checking each rock or twig. They were literally leaving no stone unturned. It was their first real crime scene for three seemingly connected murders. The first two had been washed clean by the storms, the ocean, and scavengers.

"I always wonder if there was something more I could have done. If I had stayed later every night to go over what we had."

Lettinger shook her head sadly. "It'd be nice if that were true." The agent turned back to watch. "If we work hard enough, we can stop this from happening. But we need something to work on, to work with. And we've had zilch."

Rebecca sighed and dropped her head back, staring up at the sky. The lights blotted out the stars. "I was right there. Right there. What could I have done to stop this?"

"That's a harder question to answer. But with a scene this fresh, I bet we can get time of death down to the minute."

Hoyt walked up, balancing three cups of coffee in his hands. "Logan had made us a fresh pot in the camp kitchen, right before you phoned Darian."

Rebecca grabbed one greedily. "I owe that man a steak dinner after everything he's done tonight." Ignoring the burn, she chugged the coffee.

"He won't say no, but he also won't expect it." Hoyt blew on his cup and sipped. "Bailey's checked the body over. There's no ID or identifying marks. I feel like I should know him, but right now, I'm coming up blank."

Rebecca couldn't blame him. There wasn't much of a face left.

"The techs are getting foot impressions. They found a few with good tread marks. And of course, there's the spot you found where the killer struggled with him."

"Maybe that's why the fingers were removed. He fought back and got some skin under his nails." Lettinger's inward expression betrayed the thought rolling around in her head. "It's possible these aren't related cases."

"You didn't get a good look at the cuts, did you?" Rebecca

raised her eyebrows as Lettinger shook her head, knocking her hair down into her brown eyes. "Same spot on each finger, and the cut marks look the same too. The medical examiner will have to verify that, but it feels too coincidental to me."

"That means this is most likely more related to your town than mine." Lettinger pushed her hair back and smoothed out her blouse. "We're being summoned. Let's go see what she has to say."

Rebecca turned and saw Bailey waving to them. Behind her, the corpse was being carefully tucked into a body bag.

The three of them headed over, her deputy dragging his feet even more. "Frost, how about you go check in with Darian and Locke? I want to make sure everything is secure."

"Yeah, Boss." Hoyt veered off to where the other two were still standing guard.

"When you're finished, go ahead and head home. I'm sure Angie wants to see you after running off like that."

"Rebecca, I like you, girl, but we've got to stop meeting like this." Bailey rolled her head on her neck and stretched out her arms.

"I'd much rather meet up over coffee or a nice lunch."

"Stop bringing me new bodies, and we might even find a chance to do that."

"Noted. The next one goes in the drink. Lettinger can deal with them when they end up on her shore." Rebecca jabbed her thumb at the Norfolk agent.

She seemed utterly unfazed by the hollow threat. "Eh, we're used to it there. Why do you think I get into the office so early? It's when the fishing boats go out or come in with extra parts in their nets."

"Well, we're done here. The body is just what you expected. Early to mid-twenties male, died of blunt force trauma to the face. Postmortem removal of fingers. I'll have a better idea what type of tool was used when I get him on the table."

Rebecca sighed, and Lettinger patted her on the shoulder but didn't mention her earlier warnings.

"I've got a clear schedule for now, and it's nearly three already, so I'm just going to get this done tonight. Keep an eye out for my report in the morning." Bailey leaned forward and peered into the sheriff's eyes. "But not too early. Go get some sleep. I won't be sending it over before noon at least."

"Don't hold it up on my account."

"Sure, sure." Bailey saw her people loading up the van. "We're off. Good luck."

She turned, and Rebecca noticed Ryker sitting on the edge of the crime scene. He was barely inside the lighted area. Her heart ached for him, and she went to him without thinking.

Not wanting to startle him, she called out softly as she moved toward him. "Ryker?"

His eyes were haunted as his gaze drifted over to take her in.

"Are you okay?"

"Yeah." He shook his head as he stood. "No. No, I'm not."

She stepped up beside him, brushing his shoulder with her own. "I know seeing something like that is traumatizing."

"It's not that. I mean, it is, but it also isn't. His face was gone except for his beard. Like it was pounded into his skull. I could see his brains."

Rebecca nodded. Seeing brains was somehow more grue-some than just seeing an intact corpse. "I get that."

"So I focused on the clothes instead, and Rebecca...Sheriff West, I think I know those clothes."

"You what?" She wasn't sure how she felt about him calling her by her title instead of her name.

He shifted on the wet sand. "Those clothes. I swear I saw them earlier today."

"Where? On who?"

"That's what I was trying to remember. I think I saw them at the Seafood Shack." His eyes filled with sadness. "You remember that homeless guy? The one Richmond Vale was so keen to get rid of? I bought him some fish tacos. I think your dead guy is that guy. His name was Mac."

33

Rebecca was running on fumes and coffee. She'd gone home to get some sleep, which worked until the dreams started. They'd been a disjointed mix of the recent murder victims, her parents, and Ryker having some kind of picnic on the beach. In the strange fashion of dreams, it was part party, part memorial, and part intervention for her so they could all tell her how disappointed they were in her.

After her third time snapping out of the dream, she'd given up on having a peaceful night, so she'd gone to the office to get some work done instead.

She'd put a note in the file for Hoyt to check up on Mac. He'd told her about the homeless man a few days back, but she'd never met him and didn't know his story. If he was the victim from last night, they needed to learn more about him beyond his first name.

And maybe they could find out what Richmond Vale had against the man too. Why had he wanted to get rid of him? And how far would he go to do so? Vale always struck her as a spineless, pencil-necked geek, not a person capable of smashing someone's head in with a rock.

A rock was a weapon of opportunity, and when people finally snapped, they grabbed whatever was nearby. Then, they usually freaked out and would try to hide the crime scene or flee. Sometimes, like last night, they did both.

With no motives, there was no way to exclude anyone who had any connection to the victims, no matter how small.

There's no way I could be that lucky, though. And I'm sure Vale will have a rock-solid alibi too.

Still, there was no reason not to add his name to the list, along with Andy Woodson, Lewis Chase, Wanda Chase, and Eldridge Graves. Those were the only names she had to go on for now. And the only person she hadn't connected with was Eldridge Graves.

Rebecca wrote down the address of his nursing home. A glance at the clock and some quick math showed she couldn't call there for at least an hour to schedule a visit to talk with the man. She clicked over to check her email and sighed when she saw there was still nothing from the medical examiner's office.

The sound of boots faintly echoed down the hallway. Rebecca spun in her chair and left her desk.

"Frost, is that you?"

The steps halted. "Yeah, Boss, it's me. What are you doing in early?" Hoyt's face popped around the corner to stare down the hall at her.

She shrugged and got up to meet him. "I couldn't sleep. This case is getting to me."

He pursed his lips and nodded, then headed to the coffeepot alongside her. "I get that. It was troubling me last night too. That guy seemed so familiar. It bothers me that I'd seen Mac a couple times but didn't recognize him last night."

"You saw the body for a hot second in the dark. Don't beat yourself up. We're still not positive it's this Mac person. I'm sure there was more than one man on the island last night wearing khaki shorts and a faded blue button-up."

"With hiking boots with a green-and-black pattern on them."

Rebecca nodded. "I looked the boots up. They're not exclusive, but still not something many people wear to the beach." She stirred sugar into her coffee and watched the ripples as she spoke in a lower voice. "I also went through the box of files you got me from the um, *special storage*. So far, I haven't found any link between our local problem and our recent victims."

While she trusted everyone in the office, her voice could still carry to the front door, and she didn't want to be over-heard talking about the Yacht Club. The town was still buzzing after a recent killing spree had been connected to the storied pack of elites. Instead of rumors, the islanders now had actual confirmation of the group's dirty dealings.

Hoyt turned around and leaned against the table they used as their little kitchenette. "I have to admit, I find that shocking. Three deaths that we can't find a solid connection for seems like the sort of thing they would be involved in, like the last one was. Maybe we just haven't gone through enough pages. There's still a ton more in there." He gestured with his cup to the door that led to the locker room, where a converted janitor closet held filing cabinets filled with unof-ficial records of every case the last sheriff had thought was connected to the Yacht Club and their illegal dealings.

"I did only grab some of the newer stuff, though. And Graves and Chase were out of Norfolk. The club might not be involved at all."

Hoyt looked discouraged. "I wouldn't put money on it."

She wouldn't either.

"How about we both go up to Norfolk today? Maybe you'll see something I missed. We can talk with Andy

Woodson and Wanda Chase. I'd also like to stop in and see if Eldridge Graves is up to talking. We haven't been able to get him on the phone yet, but now that the holiday is over and his nursing home is settling back down, they might be able to accommodate us."

"And pop into the state office and see if Lettinger has any matches from her missing persons list. After all, she did a great job figuring out Edmond Chase's identity just from a body description and some dental work."

"Good plan. I'm ready to go if you are."

"Fresh cup, I'm good to go. But I'm driving. You look like you're still not awake yet."

Rebecca shrugged. She'd wisely avoided looking in a mirror today and was willing to take his word for it.

They walked out together, and she plopped heavily into the passenger seat. Once her seat belt was on, she leaned back and closed her eyes. A bit more rest wouldn't be a bad thing.

Hoyt didn't say a word as he drove.

Soon, Rebecca's mind was wandering. Not to the Land of Nod, unfortunately. Instead, she mulled over everything she'd seen in her dreams last night. The past and present merging. How she'd felt about it all. She realized that, while Ryker had been in her subconscious, he hadn't always been an adult. Sometimes, he was the boy she had played with as a child instead.

The whole thing had left her feeling uneasy in her mind and soul.

She'd left the FBI and D.C. to escape the fast pace and allow herself more time to think. Things were supposed to be more straightforward. She should have known better. Hell, she'd said it herself once to a felon. There were men everywhere who thought they could get away with crimes.

Women too. Her first case involving the death of Cassie Leigh had proven that.

A simple man with a simple life thought he could get away with seducing his son's underage girlfriend, knocking her up, killing her, and leaving her body to rot in the marshes. That one act had started a domino effect that led to where she was today.

Even when conspiracies weren't involved, everything was still linked, especially on an island as small as Shadow.

How many dominos did she send tumbling just by moving down and becoming part of this town? She didn't know yet and wouldn't until all the pieces finished falling.

34

Hoyt knocked on the door of Coastal Tours while Rebecca stood behind him. He always seemed to insist on being the one to knock. She wasn't sure if it was because she was a woman or because she was his boss. This time, she let it go. Andy Woodson was standing at the counter, packing up boxes, and she didn't think they had anything to fear from the older man. So far, he'd been nothing but helpful.

"Can I help you, Deputy?" Woodson asked through the closed door.

Hoyt shifted to the side so the man could see Rebecca. "We'd like to come in and ask you a few more questions."

"Oh, Sheriff West, I didn't see you there. Come on in." He unlocked the door and pushed it open. "Are you making any more headway on Skipper's case?"

"We've had recent changes and wanted to ask you about them."

"Okay, go ahead. I hope you don't mind me working while we talk."

"Not at all."

"So what happened? Did you find the boat?"

"We did. It was wrecked on Little Quell Island."

Woodson's reaction was noticeable even if she hadn't been waiting for it. His back jerked, and his head snapped up to stare at her.

"You know Little Quell Island?"

He scratched behind his ear. "Yeah. I know it."

"It's the destination that was going to be Skipper's last charter. But it was canceled, and the entry was later erased."

"Sorry, I don't know. That is…was Skipper's business. I didn't have anything to do with the boat reservations."

Woodson was looking even more disturbed and knelt to presumably sort the stacks of paperwork at his feet.

Hoyt walked around the edge of the counter and casually leaned against it while watching the man's every move.

"But it wasn't just Skipper who used that ledger. You did too."

Woodson glanced at Hoyt, who was watching the older man like a hawk. "It was just a ledger. Just notes to help us keep track of stock. And people liked the old-fashioned aspect of signing in and out."

The deputy kept his cold eyes locked on the man as Rebecca spoke. "You had access to it and used it often. Was it you who took the reservation?"

"No, I never took reservations for the boat. Never did. Only Skipper knew when the boat would be available. Not me."

"Did you mark out that last reservation?" When Woodson's frantic movements slowed down, Rebecca knew she was right. "You did. Didn't you?"

"I might have. I don't remember." He looked frantically over his shoulder at Hoyt, then stood up and leaned over to Rebecca. Perspiration lined his lip, and he swiped at it with a shaking hand. "I would draw a line on a reservation that was canceled if I got that call. But I can't remember if I did that one."

"Would you erase a reservation?"

"No. Never. Again, that's Skipper's responsibility. And I didn't fuck with his money. He needed every cent..." His eyes widened, and he wiped at his face again.

Rebecca leaned on the counter, keeping her gaze on Woodson's face. "Well, here's what we know. We know Edmond Chase made a reservation to take his son out fishing on June twelfth. We know his son refused to go, and his name was scratched off. But not the rest. We also know that Edmond and Skipper went out and were joined by someone else, either before they left the marina or somewhere at sea. They were killed by that person, and the boat ended up wrecked on Little Quell Island. Efforts were made to make identifying them harder too. Then someone erased that entry from the log only you had access to."

Woodson's mouth worked up and down. "It wasn't me."

Rebecca's lips pinched together, and she shook her head. "It's not looking good for you, Andy. You're the only one who had access to the men, the boat, knew the reservation times, and could also erase the entry in the ledger. Plus, you would be the one to benefit when Skipper was legally declared dead. Where were you last night?"

The random question after those accusations made Woodson twitch.

"Last night? I was home alone. I'm not a fan of fireworks. Why?"

"Because another murder occurred last night. That body had some of the same disfigurements as the other corpse with Skipper had."

"Did you kill your business partner, Andy?" Hoyt stepped forward as he spoke, his thumbs tucked into his belt and his hand brushed against his holster. "Is that why he wasn't bashed over the head like Edmond Chase? Because you couldn't look him in the eye as you did it and instead wrapped him in plastic and drowned him?"

"No! Skipper was my friend. I loved him like a brother."

"Cain and Abel were brothers too," Rebecca pointed out.

The man's mouth popped open. "I'm not even going to respond to that. It's so absurd."

"I'm sorry to hear that, Andy." Rebecca thinned her lips and glanced at Hoyt.

The deputy pulled his handcuffs from his belt, letting them shake loudly.

Rebecca knew it was a bluff. They had no jurisdiction here. But with Woodson so rattled, it was a smart play by her senior deputy. "No one else had the means, motive, and opportunity to kill those men. Hoyt." She gave him the go-ahead nod.

Woodson spun away, holding up his hands. "Wait, wait, wait!"

"Wait for what? You've told us all you know, right? And so has everyone else." Rebecca gave a lazy shrug. "With the information we have, you're the only suspect. Don't worry. After the holidays, the courts usually get caught up pretty quick. You can probably get your first court date by tomorrow morning. I wouldn't count on bail…" She trailed off sadly.

Hoyt burst out laughing. "Bail. That's funny."

Woodson spun to stare at him. "What?" His shirt was soaked with sweat.

"Two deaths at sea? And a third on land linked to the first two? No judge will even consider bail. You'll be held in jail until they finish putting your court case together."

Hoyt took one step closer and reached out with the hand holding the cuffs.

"The upside of this, you've already settled things and

closed up shop." Rebecca grinned, knowing that was the last straw for him, and he was already cracking.

Woodson dodged away from the handcuffs, panting in fear. "I warned him. I told him not to go out. That it was too dangerous. But he wouldn't listen."

Now they were getting somewhere.

"Why did you warn him?"

"I don't want to talk ill of the dead." Woodson stared at the cuffs as if they were a viper ready to strike. This was not the meek, sad man she'd met before.

"It's not ill if it's the truth." Hoyt was behind him, and Woodson jerked when he saw the deputy take a second step closer.

"Skipper was a terrible poker player, but he never gave up. Even when he should have. That was the real reason he never had a wife and kids. He loved gambling more than anything except his boat."

"And how did that lead to him and Edmond Chase being killed?"

"Edmond's family runs the underground poker scene here. I don't know too much about them, but I know they're into some serious stuff. Illegal stuff I don't want to know about. They also loaned Skipper a lot of money. Not real money, but chips. All so he could keep playing. He ended up in massive debt to them after he lost it all. That was a year ago."

"If Skipper owed that much money to the Chase family, why would Edmond associate with him? From what I've learned, Edmond was trying to get away from his family business."

Woodson shook his head violently. "Get away from it? He ran it. After his old man and brother died, he took over. After Skipper got into debt, he started taking them out." He dropped his eyes. "And why I never knew when the boat would be available. Skipper was paying off his debts to the family by taking them wherever they wanted. And I don't think they were just fishing trips either."

The dots began to connect for Rebecca. Almost.

"But this last time, he'd booked a legitimate charter with Skipper to take his son out fishing. That trip on the twelfth was supposed to be the real thing."

"I don't know where you got that information, but that's not what I heard. Edmond was trying to force Lewis into going. The kid wanted nothing to do with the family business, but his dad wasn't having any of it. Skipper freaked out when he saw I'd crossed off Lewis's name. He said the old man was going to blow a gasket and hoped the boy was safe someplace outside his dad's reach."

"You make it sound like Edmond was a threat to his son." After reading about what happened over the cranberries, she didn't doubt that but wanted to see what Woodson knew.

"I don't know. That's just what Skipper said. I kept as far away from it as I could. I wanted no part in any of that. I just want to rent my stuff out to happy families so they can enjoy their vacations. Getting caught up in this mess is the last thing I ever wanted." He tapped his finger on the counter. "I will tell you this, I did not erase that entry. I don't mess with anything that isn't mine. The one thing I do know is that the entry was erased before Skipper left, and I didn't touch it."

"And how do you know that?"

"I saw Skipper put it away before he headed out. If you look at it, you can see that I used it that day too. I signed in and out with my clients. They're dated. You can check. Skipper had some entries for later dates, too, but none that were signed for. He didn't know that would be his last day on the boat. I kept writing in it past the day of his trip. If I had been the one who erased it, why would I have skipped over it to keep tracking my stuff?"

"Was anyone else with Skipper that day?"

Woodson deflated, and he looked scared again. "If I tell you, I might be a dead man too."

"Edmond Chase was here."

It wasn't a question, but he answered anyway. "Yeah. But if they find out I told you, I'm a goner. The one thing I know about the Chase family, anyone who goes against them dies."

"Andy, there is no one left of the Chase family. Edmond was the only surviving son. His wife hated her husband's family and kept her kids away from them too. His three kids don't have anything to do with the business. No one is left to come after you."

"Then who killed my buddy? Who killed Skipper?"

That was a good question. And not one she had an answer for.

"He was probably only killed because he was a witness to Edmond's murder. But with Edmond's death, it should all be over now."

Rebecca prayed her instincts were right. But if they were, why did she have another body at the morgue waiting for identification?

35

Since it was still early, Rebecca decided the best person to talk to next was Eldridge Graves. As they pulled up to the facility, Hoyt whistled and ducked his head to get a better look at the enormous building. Rebecca rechecked the address and name to ensure she had the right one.

"Are you sure this is the right place?" She stared out the window at the vast gardens and perfectly manicured lawns.

"This is the one. Talked to the manager and his nurse myself. They wouldn't let me talk to Eldridge because phones tend to spook him."

"In light of Skipper's bank records, this seems a bit excessive, doesn't it?" Rebecca climbed out of the Explorer and shut the door as she continued to look around. There were shade trees and little benches everywhere. She could see walking trails used by residents, some with attendants walking alongside them.

"Not sure. But I'd bet it's outside of my budget, no matter how much I loved my brother." Rebecca saw Hoyt look around, too, taking in the expansive windows and artistically shaped bushes.

The double front doors were on a wide concrete porch with stately white columns lining it. Hoyt pulled the door open and held it for her.

As Rebecca stepped inside, a woman in a double-breasted white jacket and matching slacks hurried over.

"Are you Sheriff West?" She spoke in a hushed voice and waved a hand to direct them away from the front lobby, which was full of elderly patients.

Not wanting to cause any upset and seeing several confused eyes already locked on her, Rebecca followed behind the woman with a nod. Upsetting patients was the last thing she wanted to do. They remained silent until they were led into a consultation room, and the door was closed gently behind them.

"You're here about Eldridge Graves? I spoke to one of your deputies about him earlier." She pulled a phone out of her pocket and sent a text. "I'm Dorothy Lassiter, administrative assistant for Mr. Lake."

Rebecca shook Ms. Lassiter's hand. "This is Deputy Frost. You spoke to him earlier, and yes. We would like to speak to Eldridge if he's up for it."

"He's been told about his brother's death, but he's not accepting it. He may never accept it. If he talks about his brother in the present tense, please do not correct him." Another staff member stepped in quickly, closing the door behind him. "This is my boss, Dean Lake, the manager here. He can explain further."

Mr. Lake nodded to Ms. Lassiter, who took that as her dismissal and hurried out of the room. He reached out to shake their hands. "Sheriff West? Thank you for waiting. Eldridge, like most of our residents, does not handle change well. Or the excitement and noise that comes from loud holidays. We appreciate you waiting this long to speak with him.

But I'm not certain what you're going to be able to learn. He has fairly advanced Alzheimer's."

"We're hoping he can tell us anything about his brother or his business that might help our investigation." Rebecca kept her words as neutral as possible as he led them out of the room and down a long hall. "In case you're worried about him, we have no plans to grill him about anything. We just want to learn as much as possible about his brother, Samuel."

"Well, I can tell you that Eldridge called him Skipper, and he visited nearly every week after he managed to get Eldridge into our facility. I can also say without a doubt that Skipper loved his older brother very much. In fact, Skipper prepaid for two years of Eldridge's stay." Lake's expression dissolved into a mask of worry. "I'm not sure what will happen to him at the end of the year."

"When did Eldridge come here?"

"About eighteen months ago. He's made great progress with us too. In fact, today, he's fairly lucid and chatty." Lake pushed open an exterior door. "But that can change at any moment."

Rebecca considered the timeline. Skipper was doing well enough eighteen months ago to prepay for two years of care in this expensive home. Had that caused him to run out of money only six months later? Was that why he'd started the gambling that led him to working his debt off with the Chase family a year ago?

Lake approached an elderly man sitting on a bench. He was wearing a bathrobe, but it was clean and wrinkle-free. In his hands, he held crackers, which he was crumbling up and tossing at his feet. The birds and squirrels that had been gathered around him scattered as the small group approached.

Eldridge turned and scowled up at them until he saw Lake's face. "My old friend, what are you doing here?"

He leaned over with one hand extended and Lake caught him before he could tumble onto the ground.

Lake shook the hand that still had bits of cracker in it, and got the man righted again. "Hello, Eldridge. I wanted to introduce you to two new friends. They know your brother and want to talk to you about him."

"My brother?" The elderly man's eyebrows came together and formed a tree of wrinkles before they relaxed and stretched away into a delighted grin. "Skipper! My brother. He's a good man. My favorite brother too." He chuckled to himself.

Rebecca laughed as well. She knew Skipper was Eldridge's only brother.

"Is Skipper here? It's been so long since I've seen him."

"No, he couldn't make it today."

"Figures. He's always so caught up with those new friends of his. He used to visit me every day before." His lips puckered, and his eyes wandered off as a bird bravely hopped forward.

"He got new friends?"

"That's what he called them. But they didn't seem too friendly to me. He says I shouldn't say things like that because they helped him get me in here, but he always seems so edgy when he talks about them. I didn't like that. I told him he should find better friends."

"Why didn't you think they were good enough to be friends with your brother?"

"They like to hide stuff. Keep stuff from him. He says that. And he never tells me what it is. He always told me all about his boating trips before. But now he doesn't. He won't take me out, either, which isn't fair. He told Mom that he'd take me fishing for my eighteenth birthday, but he still isn't back from his last trip with those new friends of his. I don't like them. If he doesn't hurry up, he won't make it. And I'll have to go out fishing on my own."

"When was the last time you saw him?" Rebecca waited patiently for the man to process her question.

"It was…last time…I have a calendar I mark his visits on." He pulled a small notebook from his pocket and began thumbing through the pages. "We sat in the window and watched the cardinals. They're my favorite birds. You can always see them so good in the winter. The males, at least. The females are darker and blend in with the branches, so they can protect the babies."

"So it was the winter?"

"What was the winter?"

Rebecca took a calming breath. "What did you write in your calendar? When did your brother last visit you?"

Eldridge flipped through a few pages, but from her vantage point, they all appeared to be covered in doodles. If it was a calendar, it only made sense to Eldridge.

"Did Skipper tell you that he was going to—"

"You know Skipper?" he asked with a cheerful, childlike smile. "How is he these days? It's been so long since I've seen him."

Rebecca glanced at Lake, who shook his head slightly, indicating she should wait.

Eldridge went back to staring at the trees. "I like the blue jays the best. They're so pretty and loud. You can always hear them singing."

36

"Should we go ahead and check in with the Chase family now, or do you want to get lunch first?"

They hadn't been able to get any more information out of Eldridge. The poor man had fallen into a cycle of forgetting and repeating. Mr. Lake didn't even need to ask them to leave before they gave an excuse and left Eldridge to go back to his bird friends.

Hoyt frowned and shook his head. "I'd rather not think about lunch at the moment. Seeing that poor man continually forgetting that his brother was dead turned my stomach."

Rebecca didn't want to admit that she felt the same way. Forever missing his brother and yet still aware that it had been a long time since his last visit was a terrible way to live.

"I think it might be your heart that's aching, not your stomach."

"Either or both. But I'd rather do something else than sit around and eat with his lost voice still in my head like this."

"It's the Sunday of a weekend holiday. Wanda and the younger sons might still be at home. Let's see if they're up to having another chat." She punched the Chase address into the GPS.

Sure enough, when they pulled up in front of Wanda Chase's house, her car was parked there, and the front door was standing open with only the screen door closed.

Hoyt knocked on the aluminum door, creating a loud, thumping rattle.

"Who is it?" a woman's voice called from the kitchen.

"Mrs. Chase, it's Sheriff West again."

Wanda rushed out and pushed open the door. It wasn't even five o'clock, well, anywhere yet, but the smell of alcohol was thick on her breath.

"Do you have any more information about my husband?"

"May we come in?"

"Yes. Yes, of course. Sorry. Don't...don't mind the mess." She swept through the front room, scooping up bottles that used to hold beer and liquor. "The boys and I had a rough few nights of it. They're not handling this well."

Rebecca ignored the alcohol, even though a part of her wondered if the high school senior had been drinking. This family had enough to worry about with her adding underage consumption to the mix. "I can't imagine they would be, losing their father like this."

Wanda gestured at the sofa. "Please, sit. Would you like something to drink? Coffee? Soda?"

Rebecca didn't really want coffee but hoped Wanda would join her in a cup and sober up a little. While booze did help numb the pain somewhat, it did not speed up the grieving process. She knew that from her own experiences. "I would love a cup."

Hoyt shook his head and waved off the offer when Wanda turned to where he was still standing by the door. With a decisive nod, she went into the kitchen. There a loud rattle of glass as she threw the bottles away and quickly returned with two cups of coffee on a little silver tray with cream and a sugar bowl. She must have had it set up already to bring it back so quickly. Probably ready for other guests that always showed up after the announcement of someone's death.

"Any updates?"

"We found the *Chum Runner*, the boat your husband was scheduled to take on June twelfth. It was on Little Quell Island."

Wanda melted into the recliner, as if her legs had turned to putty.

Rebecca and Hoyt both darted forward to catch the tray before she burned herself.

Hoyt took the coffees and set them on the table, then mixed one with heavy cream and sugar and passed the cup to the shocked woman.

"He was still hoping Lewis would come join him." Tears welled in Wanda's eyes. "My husband died thinking our oldest son hated him."

Rebecca picked up her cup and took a sip while staring at Wanda. The woman mimicked her movements like she'd hoped and took a gulp of her own.

"We've also had another murder. This time on our island. We believe it's linked to your husband's death."

"My husband was killed weeks ago out at sea. How could he have anything to do with this?"

"That's what we're here to find out. Do you know if your husband had any reason to visit Shadow Island?"

Wanda shook her head, eyes still glassy from shock, and took another drink. "Nothing I can think of. That's one of the barrier islands, right? The only reason he would go down that way would be to fish. But he never fished on land. Only on the boats. It was his favorite hobby."

"Oh, I bet that was annoying. I know fishing equipment

can be expensive. Especially the deep-sea gear. That had to cost a pretty good amount."

Wanda slowly turned her head to stare up at Hoyt as he spoke, and she frowned. "I'm not sure. I never saw any equipment. I think he rented that from the marina too. He never brought any home."

Rebecca raised an eyebrow but tried to get her face back to neutral before Wanda Chase noticed. Skipper didn't rent out fishing equipment. Not rods or anything like that, at least. She'd looked at plenty of pictures of his outings by now. The only fishing gear he had on his boat was a gaff and a net pole. And Woodson didn't rent those out either. Otherwise, that would have shown up in the ledger.

"Well, it can take a while to get a set. How long has he been fishing?"

"He took it up after his father died. When I asked him about it, he said it was his way to remember the good times with his dad. I wasn't going to stop him from doing that. Especially not since he was so bad at it." She laughed raggedly. "You know, in all the years and all the trips he took, he never once brought home a fish. He'd tell me about what he caught and say he released it. And there were never any pictures either. Just a few of him and the boys posing on the boat or the dock."

"You mentioned his father's death before. Can you tell me what happened?"

"I can tell you what I read in the paper. Or…hold on a moment." Wanda set her cup down and walked off down the hall toward the bedrooms. There were a few thumps, and then she returned, carrying a thick scrapbook.

"Edmond kept this. Said it helped him stay connected to his roots." She flipped the cover open, and they could see newspaper clippings, awards, ribbons, pictures, and even a few tickets to concerts. "Here it is."

She spun the scrapbook around on the table and pointed at an article. "Father and Son Dumped in River."

"What can you tell me about the brother?" Rebecca looked up at Wanda, who was rolling her lips between her teeth.

"Marcus. Edmond's older brother. He never spoke about Marcus at all. I didn't even know he had a brother until the man died." She tapped the clipping next to the article. "This is his obituary. That's all I know about him. Wish they'd added a photograph."

Another brother who was killed because of the family business. Why hadn't Edmond learned from his father's mistakes and stayed out of it?

"Would you mind if I take a picture of this?"

Wanda shook her head and pulled off the protective plastic so Rebecca could get a good shot. "Have you found my boy? Lewis? I can't get in touch with him, but you're the police. You must have more resources to track him down than I do."

Rebecca shook her head and put her phone away. "No, ma'am. But we're still looking."

"Only thing that might help is he emptied out his savings on the same day as the boat outing. I still get his mail."

Rebecca sat taller. "June twelfth?"

Wanda nodded. "Please, find my boy. If I need to report him missing, I will. Just find my son. He needs to know about his father. And his brothers need their big brother to help them through this tough time." She stared wistfully up at the pictures. "They're adults now, but they're still so young. Too young to have to deal with losing their father."

Rebecca wanted to agree with her. Losing a parent was hard, no matter the age.

37

"Sheriff West, good to see you again. Any chance I can talk you two into another working lunch?" Rhonda Lettinger gestured at the menu as they sat down across the table from her.

She laughed as Hoyt reached across her to grab one. When they'd called to see if they could reach Lettinger, the dispatcher called her. They learned she was enjoying her holiday weekend by having lunch down the block. She asked them to join her there, since she was trying to steer clear of the office if she could help it.

There were already two glasses of water and two coffees set out for them when they arrived. Lettinger was drinking the same thing. It made sense, considering none of them got much sleep the night before.

"I could learn to like working with you." Rebecca glanced down at the menu and, as soon as she saw the meatloaf sandwich, she knew what she was going to get.

"What am I? Chopped liver? I fed you my wife's famous five-cheese noodles."

Rebecca shrugged as she downed half her glass of water.

"But I already like working with you. She's still in progress."

"Are you saying food is the way to a good working relationship with you?" Lettinger grinned at the banter.

"I'm saying I prefer that my jobs allow me the ability to eat during the day. With food better than I would get from a vending machine."

Hoyt didn't even look up as he kept perusing the selections. "Oh, don't let Lilian hear you say that. She'll end up making you fat."

"Lilian? Darian's wife?" Rebecca looked at him, puzzled.

"Yeah. She's a foodie and likes trying out new recipes. To her credit, she's a great cook, even if she does make the most random things. If she finds out that you're always hungry at work, she'll start bringing in her latest..." Hoyt stared at Rebecca as she pulled out her phone and started typing. "What are you doing?"

"Messaging Darian to ask for Lilian's contact information so I can tell her I will happily be a guinea pig for her creations." Her message sent, she looked up to find two pairs of eyes staring at her with amusement. "What?"

"The question now is, will your deputy, Darian, be happy or mad at having to share his wife's culinary innovations?" Lettinger smirked, then looked up as the server approached.

"Both." Hoyt sighed before placing his lunch order.

Rebecca waited 'til they'd all ordered, then broached the topic that had brought them together.

"Have you been able to find out where Lewis Chase disappeared to?"

"No, not yet. I can say he didn't rent any moving vans or vehicles. He doesn't have a car of his own, so he didn't drive. I did learn that he didn't renew or transfer his license. DMV up there is slow, but not this slow. At least that's what they insist. He also didn't get a bus, plane, or train ticket out. If he caught a ride or hitchhiked, we're out of luck tracking that."

"What about the Colorado Bureau of Investigation?" Rebecca asked.

"I reached out to CBI and have them digging as well, in case he did, in fact, hitchhike. The problem with that is, I can't find any friends or acquaintances of his that live there. His last credit card use was in mid-June. That's also when he emptied his bank account. June twelfth."

Rebecca wished Lettinger had better news.

"What do you know about Marcus Chase?"

"Marcus?"

"Edmond Chase's older brother. He died about ten years ago."

"Oh, yeah, that guy. I forgot about him. Nothing on him. He was a nobody. His name never came up in anything crime-related. He must have been with his father the night he was killed, but that's about the only thing that ever happened with him. That's the only reason he would matter to anyone that I know of."

"Do you know of any connection between the Chase family and Shadow Island?"

"Boats. That's about it. They worked with some club down there and used their boats to move their products around. Drugs and small firearms, mostly. Underground poker too. But they would also move people around, usually the ones trying to hide from cops. We never learned the name of the club, though, just that it was a boat club."

"That is the name of the club. It's called the Yacht Club and it's run out of the Seaview Marina on Shadow Island."

Lettinger snorted and pulled out a notebook to take notes. "That's a stupid name. Like having a biker club and calling it the Bike Club. Or naming your cat 'Cat.'"

"Couldn't agree more. But that might have been their intention. To keep the name as generic as possible so no one would think to look into them. Their name is the only thing about them that isn't flashy."

"Interesting."

Rebecca decided to take a risk. "They're known to traffic in sex slaves, drugs, and anything else that can make them money. And they're bankrolled by some of the über-wealthy and influential. Which is why, so far, we haven't been able to make a case stick against them."

"The kind where I have to be careful about who I talk to when asking about them?" Lettinger seemed to have caught on quickly. "Because that would explain the weird responses I get every time I look into this unnamed club."

"That would be a good idea. Be careful."

"Nothing like making my job harder." She sighed and continued taking notes.

When Lettinger wasn't watching, Hoyt gave Rebecca a look. He was even warier about sharing any information on the Yacht Club than she was. Rebecca nodded, letting him know she wouldn't go any further. Not yet at least.

"Have you made any headway on officially identifying your newest John Doe?" Lettinger finished writing.

"Not yet. It's going to be the same slog as before. Running dental records and DNA to look for a possible match. But those, as we know, take time. We have a possible name, Mac, but no last name or any way to know if that was his real name and not just his street name. Waiting for a call back from his landlady."

"Good. Once you have something, let me know, and I'll check my missing persons files. This could be another one of our people ending up on your shores."

"Which reminds me, you might want to reach out to Wanda Chase. She's thinking of filing a report on her son, Lewis."

"I'll call her again first thing tomorrow morning."

38

R ebecca took a long drink of her coffee. It was tepid from sitting so long, but that didn't matter to her. She was using it as a means of staying awake as she flipped through another paper.

The rest of the day had been mostly uneventful. There was a report for possible shots fired out by the old lighthouse. When Hoyt and Darian went to check, it turned out to be some idiot with a string of firecrackers. He'd been sent on his way with a stern talking-to and nothing more.

On his way back, Hoyt had finally gotten a return call from the hostel owner, so he let Rebecca know he was going to stop in there before he came back to help go through the paperwork.

Banker's boxes were stacked on and around Rebecca's desk, and she'd been meticulously going through them. These were the files Wallace had stored, but never filed or sorted at all. Now that she was going through them, she saw no reason not to do so properly.

On her computer screen, she had the bank statements for

Samuel Graves and Edmond Chase pulled up. She'd planned on comparing them to each other but found something more interesting in the older paperwork that sent her down a rabbit hole of research.

"What the hell, Boss?" Hoyt stepped over the stacks of papers. "Did a paper bomb go off in here?"

"Before I answer that," Rebecca moved some files to the side that she wanted to go through later, "tell me what you found out."

"Mac, as I knew him, was registered under the name Mac Chandler and he's been there since June twentieth." He sat in the chair and rested his feet on the box she'd left in front of it.

"Mac is what he registered with? Sounds like an alias. They didn't run a check on him?"

Hoyt's shoulders twitched in a lazy shrug. "Could have been a nickname. But no, they didn't see the point. He paid cash and didn't bother anyone. He also had a security deposit."

"Things are starting to make a little bit of sense to me now."

"How so?" His eyes roamed over the mess she'd made in his absence.

"June twelfth was the day Lewis Chase emptied out his bank accounts, according to his mom."

Hoyt paused and frowned. "You think the two men have something to do with each other?"

"I think the two men might actually be one man. When Lewis Chase left his family, I bet he took a different name. He gave up being a Chase and tried to become an ordinary guy. I never met Mac, but I did find pictures of Lewis when he was a bit younger. Could this be him?"

She turned one of the papers she'd held out so he could look at the picture on it.

"Maybe…but his jawline is different. Even with that big beard, Mac doesn't quite look like Lewis."

"The Lewis from the picture maybe. But after his fight with his father, he had to get reconstructive surgery on his jaw. After that, he spent a lot less time with his family and never posted pictures of himself online. In fact, it seemed he didn't like having his picture taken at all after his surgery."

"Yeah, I could see that. If my old man messed my face up so bad it didn't look the same, I wouldn't want to see it again either." He rubbed his thumb across his temple and up his eyebrow.

Rebecca kept her gaze away from the old, mostly faded scar that resided there.

"I told Bailey about my theory and she's going to run a paternity test. We already DNA-typed Edmond's body when he was a John Doe. It should be easy enough to check if they're related." Rebecca shuffled some papers. "That's not the only strange coincidence I found in our timeline."

Hoyt cleared his throat before he pulled himself up straight in his chair. "There's more?"

"You remember how I got that copy of the Seaview Marina's rental history?"

"From the Robert Leigh case? Yeah, you found it in Jake Underwood's home office." Now she really had his attention. He dropped his feet to the floor so he could lean forward.

"The day after Marcus Chase was supposedly shot and dumped in the river alongside his father, Michael Smith rented out a slip here at the Seaview Marina."

Hoyt leaned back slightly. "Wait, Michael Smith? Do you mean Mike?"

Rebecca held up a hand. "Hang with me on this. We'll circle back to the name in a minute."

"Okay. So Michael Smith rented a slip at the marina? I

mean the dates line up, but plenty of people died that same day. People die every day."

"Here's where it gets interesting. Only one body was ever recovered. They assumed Marcus's body was carried away from the wreck but not the father's because he was wearing a seat belt. And then there's this tidbit. After Edmond got married and had his first child, he was given a monthly stipend. It came from his father's account and increased slightly with every child they had."

"So grandpa was giving his grandchildren money every month? Taking care of his family. Nothing too strange about that. Maybe he was setting up a college fund for the kids."

"Or a paycheck from the family business. Which wouldn't be too strange. Except it kept coming after his father and older brother supposedly died." Rebecca grinned. "Same amount, but from a different account."

"Which you traced to Michael Smith?"

"Which I traced to Michael Smith. Funny thing, though, Michael Smith doesn't have a driver's license or car registered to his name."

Hoyt tapped his temple. "Where have I heard that story before?"

"We also don't have a mugshot because he was never arrested for anything. Until I do more digging, I only have this one picture from his obituary." She turned on her phone and flipped it around to show him. "Do you know any new, upper-crust Michael Smiths who've moved here in the last ten years or so?"

Hoyt took the phone from her, and his fingers clenched around the case. "Not a one."

Rebecca was surprised. From his reaction, she was certain he'd recognized the man in the photo.

"But I know a middle-class 'Mike Smith' that has that exact same scar on his forearm."

Her heart rate increased. "You know him? Any chance you know where he lives?"

He looked up at the clock and stood. "I can do you one better. I know where he's at right now."

39

"That's the last of them." I wiped my brow and walked over to lean against the soda dispenser. It was nice and cool in the corner next to the ice machine, a perfect place to get away from the heat of the fryers.

Guy Ragsdill glanced up from chopping a tomato. "I hope the rest of the summer isn't this packed every day. I could hardly keep all the orders straight in my head." Though Guy had worked for me the last two summers, he was slow with a knife.

I forced a laugh, intent on keeping up with the jovial persona I'd bullshitted the islanders with for the past ten years. "Don't give me that shit. You've been working here long enough that you could do this in your sleep."

He mimed flipping a fryer and assembling a taco, adding a little snore for what he accessed was humor. "I guess so. What about you?"

"Between the catering, the construction crews, the shack on the beach, and yesterday's constant demands, I feel like I've been doing this in my sleep too."

Guy stopped chopping. "At least you got to enjoy the fireworks last night, unlike the rest of us."

Was the little bitch pouting? Worse, I didn't like that he knew which hours I'd been away.

"That's why I'm the boss."

"Well, it was our busiest night of the summer, and you just bailed. Didn't you say it was supposed to be all hands on deck for the party?"

Snowflake didn't like that answer. Though I wanted to punch him, I shrugged and put on my most contrite expression. I was the boss, but it didn't hurt to appear humble. "Sorry, man. I had a family medical emergency. My brother's kid fell and hit his head. It was really bad. There was blood all over. I had to stay with him and hold his hand. His mom was a wreck." I played it up, as if I'd been disturbed by what I'd seen and the pain the child had gone through.

It worked like a charm. The boy was immediately contrite. "Oh shit, man. I'm sorry. If I'd known, I wouldn't have given you a hard time over it. Is he gonna be okay?"

I shook my head sadly as I poured myself a glass of soda. "Well, his nose is never going to be the same, but other than that, it's a wait-and-see thing. You know how tricky head wounds can be."

It wasn't just a busy time for the Seafood Shack, it was also a busy time for me to be running product in and out under cover of the tourists. Having a "sick" nephew as a premade excuse could be a good thing. In the end, the worthless brat might at least make for a handy alibi.

He certainly hadn't been any good at fighting. Or wrestling. The kid didn't have the gumption to make anything of himself on his own. Cracking his skull open had probably been a mercy kill for someone like him.

"Look, man, if you need anything, just let me know. I can

cover for a couple of hours if you need to be with him." Guy walked around to comfort me but stopped as the sound of doors closing in the parking lot reached them. "Aw, man, I thought the dinner rush wasn't going to start for a bit."

Thankful for the distraction—now I didn't have to endure the awkward shoulder pats Guy was about to apply—I walked up to the window to see who it was.

Two cop cars were parked in the lot. That was strange enough. But Sheriff West and Deputy Hoyt were talking something over. When they stopped talking, they both reached down and unsnapped their guns from their holsters.

Adrenaline ran through my muscles like a cold waterfall. There was only one reason cops would do that, then casually walk up to a place. They were trying to take me by surprise.

"Actually, Guy, there is one thing I need of you."

"Sure, Mike, anything."

He never even looked down as I reached for the kitchen shears that I kept in my apron to cut the crabs and lobsters. "I need you to be a distraction so I can get away."

Guy frowned in confusion, then his face twisted in pain as I stabbed the razor-sharp shears deep into his lower body, giving them a good upward thrust to create the most damage possible. I clapped my hand over his mouth and sank to the floor with him as blood poured out and his legs grew weak. The cops hadn't seen us yet. I needed him to distract the cops, not call them over sooner.

It would be close, but if they both went to save Guy, then I could make a clean getaway. I would find a new island and start all over again with a new name. That wasn't hard in my line of work, and I already had a new one picked out and ready to assume.

But first, I had to lose these cops. Or kill them, if they got too close.

I looked down at Guy's wide, tear-filled eyes and smiled as I wrapped my hands around my trusty shears once more. "This is gonna hurt, so you should scream really loud for me."

40

W hen a scream of mortal pain came from the Seafood Shack, Rebecca froze, but only for a second. Hand on her weapon, she advanced toward the sound, only stopping when a door slammed somewhere in the back of the small building.

The puzzle pieces clicked together at once.

"He's running!"

Hoyt faltered, his eyes wide in indecision.

"Go assist the person screaming and call for backup," Rebecca yelled over her shoulder as she sprinted to the side of the restaurant, scanning the area for their perp.

There!

She'd only caught a flash of blue shirt as a man scampered behind another building, but she knew he was their man. She took off, rounding the corner just as her suspect ducked down an adjacent street.

"This is the sheriff," she called in her command voice. "Stop running!"

At times like these, she found it ridiculous that she had to announce herself to a man who knew her identity, but many cases had been lost in court because the suspect "didn't know the police were chasing" him.

Better safe than looking like a dumbass on the witness stand.

Scanning the street names, she drew a mental map of the island. In only a few weeks, she still didn't know every inch of its twenty-eight square miles, but she'd studied the roadways until she knew them by heart. This was familiar. Instead of following him, she took the next street over, knowing they ran parallel. She did, however, miscalculate how busy that particular sidewalk would be.

Dammit.

"Sheriff's department. Move!"

Tourists of all shapes and sizes dodged out of her way, but she was forced to weave around the ones who shifted too slowly. Those who didn't move fast enough were grabbed by other civilians and yanked out of her way as her feet pounded the concrete.

This was why she always insisted on wearing running shoes or sneakers instead of boots or dressier footwear. Like this, she could keep up with almost any criminal. And she was. She could see him through the alleys that ran between the two streets. In fact, even with the obstacles she'd faced, she was gaining on him. When he glanced over his shoulder, she got a clear view of his face.

Mike.

It was Michael Smith, owner of the Seafood Shack. The man had been right under their noses the entire time. That pissed her off.

The damn man still wore his white chef's apron, though it was now splattered with blood.

This man had been killing people, then coming to work as cool as a cucumber and serving their neighbors their lunches. He had to have ice in his veins.

A delivery van came down the street, and Rebecca lost her target for a moment. She spotted him a second later, cutting across the street in front of her. He was moving faster, both arms pumping.

So was she.

A family blocked the sidewalk in front of him while a bread truck barricaded the street. For a terrible moment, Rebecca was sure Smith would grab the baby stroller, securing himself a hostage.

Don't do it.

As if he'd heard her, he turned right instead, down an alley filled with debris. His hand dove into a pocket, but there was no way to tell if he was reaching for a weapon, because a second later, he smashed through a stack of cardboard boxes.

Rebecca pulled her Springfield. "Michael Smith, this is the sheriff. Stop and put down your weapon."

He didn't, of course.

Jumping a box, she followed him down the alley, grateful to see a fence blocking the exit. Would he try to scale it, or would he turn around and face her?

She had to be ready for anything.

"Michael Smith, this is the sheriff. Stop and put your hands in the air."

Smith didn't slow as he closed in on the obstacle. He jumped, his hands reaching for the top of the fence. Her question of whether he was armed was answered as light glinted off the blade in his right hand.

That was okay. She'd brought a gun to a knife fight.

Within seconds, she sighted her Springfield on him. *Shit.* Rebecca was a lot of things, but she wouldn't shoot a person in the back. And despite being encumbered by the knife in his hand, fast and agile, he was up and over the fence.

Holstering her weapon, she took off, ready to scale the

fence. She hated how vulnerable this would make her but moved as quickly as she could. Catching the top of the fence with her palms, she cursed as the new skin tore, but didn't let that stop her as she vaulted over the top.

On her feet with weapon in hand once again, she looked right and left.

Where'd the fucker go?

She caught sight of him heading past the business district. He seemed to be aiming toward a small pier near the eastern edge of the island. She holstered the gun and took off.

Did he have a boat stashed there? If so, she needed to catch up with him before he reached it. Smith was a big man, not just tall but wide as well. Most of it seemed to be muscle from the way he was moving. She could probably bring him down with a tackle, but then she'd have a fight on her hands once she got him on the ground.

That was okay with her.

Triggering her mic, she radioed in her current location and a description of Michael Smith. "He's carrying a knife, so consider him armed and dangerous."

He cut a path through the backyard of a small house, and she was right behind him, listening as Viviane called in her coordinates to the others. Smith threaded his way between two cars that slammed on their brakes with a screech.

She, on the other hand, didn't have to slow down as the cars were already coming to a stop. Rebecca slid across the hood of a shiny blue Mustang, saving her precious seconds. She was only feet away now.

Smith hit the softer soil on the side of the road right before the sand started.

Now!

As his foot shifted, he leaned forward to keep his balance.

Rebecca lunged, wrapping her arms around his biceps to

pin his arms by his sides. The sudden weight threw him off balance, and he crashed to the ground with her on top.

He was a fighter, though, and knew what he was doing. Even as he hit the ground, he tucked and rolled. Once he was a few feet away, he lashed out with the blade.

Having anticipated the move, Rebecca pulled her weapon, backing up even farther to create more distance.

"Do you really want to do this?"

She was pleased by how much command was still in her voice after their long sprint, and by how little her hands shook. She did not want to convey fear, not to this bastard.

"You bitch."

She put her sights on center mass. "I will shoot you if you don't drop that knife in three seconds."

She didn't count. She didn't need to. Just like most bullies, Michael Smith didn't enjoy being on the receiving end. Rebecca saw the surrender in his eyes before his fingers opened and the knife dropped to the ground.

"Take three big steps backward and lower yourself to the ground, hands behind your head."

Watching him closely, sights still on his chest, she didn't inhale a deep breath until he was facedown on the ground. Still, she didn't trust him.

Leading with her gun, she came up behind him, pressing the barrel into the back of his neck until she got a knee into his spine. She smiled as she popped open the new pouch and pulled out a set of handcuffs. Seconds later, Michael Smith, or rather Marcus Chase, was secured.

Exhaling a long breath, she began reading the asshole his rights.

41

Rebecca flipped through the pages of everything they'd learned about their suspect. It wasn't much, but she'd filled her file full of miscellaneous papers to thicken it a bit. It was always a good idea to make a suspect think you knew much more than you actually did.

Darian shifted, making himself more comfortable against the wall behind their suspect. Rebecca wondered if his duty belt needed to be adjusted. Maybe she should buy each of her deputies one just like hers.

Hers was comfortable, especially considering it weighed nearly thirty pounds. While she'd been running after Chase, she'd been impressed with how well the weight was distributed and how easy it'd been to access everything.

She started a list of all the things she needed to purchase for her deputies, making sure that Marcus Chase couldn't see what she was writing. Let him wonder. Let him sweat. Let the silence eat away at him.

"If you expect me to crack under whatever it is you're doing, I will not. Silence doesn't bother me."

Rebecca raised her head, acting like she'd forgotten there

was someone else in the room. Apparently, the silence did bother him. Otherwise, he wouldn't have seen the need to fill it. She ran a finger down the page she was pretending to read. "Then shut up and let me read in peace. You do have the right to remain silent, remember."

She could see him through her lashes and idly wondered if she should get bangs. It was something she'd pondered off and on for most of her career. If watching bad guys squirm through her lashes worked, having an extra fringe of hair would only make it easier. The only downside she could think of would be having to maintain such short hair.

When she was a teenager, she'd once made the mistake of trying to cut her own hair and ended up looking like...well... she didn't want to think about that particularly embarrassing time in her life. Needless to say, she'd sworn off bangs forever.

"What?" Chase sneered. "Did you get to the juicy part? Is that why you're making that disgusted face? To try to convince me that you know what a bad man I am? It won't work."

"No, actually. Your file is so damn boring that my mind wandered, and I was debating a change of hairstyle, but then I remembered how bad I looked in bangs. Have you ever tried to trim your own bangs? You know, back when you had hair. If you had, you'd understand why I was making that face."

She met his gaze, letting him see the truth of her words. For once, she wasn't even lying and could use that to her advantage.

His sneer melted away as Darian laughed behind his back.

Rebecca crossed her arms and leaned back in her chair. "If you want to be so chatty and refuse to let me read, then why don't you tell me about yourself instead, Mr. Smith? Or should I just skip the bullshit and call you Marcus Chase?"

He yanked at the cuffs bolted to the table. "Guess that's for you to figure out."

She laughed. "I've already done that."

His nostrils flared. "Really? What do you think you know?"

Rebecca laced her fingers together. "You're Marcus Chase, older brother to Edmond Chase and head of the Chase crime family. You killed your father ten years ago and faked your own death."

She was half guessing at that last part, but the brief widening of his eyes told her she was on the right track.

"After you killed your father and disappeared, you came to Shadow Island to start up your own syndicate under an alias."

One side of his mouth lifted in disgust. "And your idiot deputies never once noticed anything. Guess they're as stupid as you."

She smiled. "If I'm so stupid, why don't you enlighten me?"

He narrowed his eyes. "I will when my lawyer is sitting beside me."

Dammit.

Rebecca picked up a random page to hide a flicker of disappointment. She'd expected him to lawyer up immediately, and wondered why he hadn't. "Are you asking for an attorney? That actually surprises me. You don't seem to be the kind of man who hides behind others."

"I don't hide behind anyone."

Her attempt to goad him worked. She lifted an eyebrow. "You hid behind a chef's apron for a long time, so please don't take offense when I laugh in your face about that."

Chase's cheeks reddened, and the handcuffs clinked when he pulled them again. "You don't know who you're dealing with. I'd be very careful if I were you."

She leaned forward. "Then why don't you tell me?"

Rebecca watched him sort through his options and dismiss them one by one. She'd already diagnosed him as a malignant narcissist and would bet her new duty belt that he wouldn't be able to stop himself from talking, thinking himself smarter than her.

Would he tell her the truth or lie, though? With a malignant narcissist, it could go either way.

"You're wrong about my father."

"Really?"

"I didn't kill him. He was weak and let a rival gang infiltrate our family."

That could actually be true.

"So this rival gang killed your father? Did they try to kill you too?"

His dark eyes narrowed. "They tried and failed."

"But instead of going back to the family, you changed your name and hid."

He yanked harder at the chains, and Rebecca was glad they'd also shackled his ankles. She had no doubt he'd try to kick her if he could.

"I didn't hide."

She laughed, knowing the sound would be like fingernails on a chalkboard to him. "I think your apron tells a different story."

His teeth squeaked from where he gritted them so hard. "I took advantage of a situation by declaring myself dead. I took the win and started a new life where I could move unencumbered by my family's history. Once here, I took my knowledge and rebuilt an even more lucrative business." He leaned forward. "Right under your nose."

"So the Seafood Shack was just a way to launder money? What happened to your brother? Did he discover you were alive, and you had to kill him?"

Chase laughed. "I don't know what you're talking about."

She let it go for now. "What about your nephew? Does everyone who learns of your secret have to die?"

His smile grew wider. "Who? You mean that homeless bum on the beach?"

"Yes…him. The one with your hair in his hand."

It was a lie, but she enjoyed the flicker of fear that crossed Marcus Chase's face immensely.

"He attacked me while I was watching the fireworks."

Behind Chase, Darian smiled. They might not have enough evidence to pin Edmond Chase or Skipper's murder on him yet, but this admission gave them yet another charge to toss his way.

"Let me see if I have everything straight." She lifted one finger. "Your nephew attacked you last night, and then," she lifted a second finger, "your employee at the Shack attacked you today? Two murdered in less than twenty-four hours. Seems two is your favorite number."

Before coming into the interrogation room, Rebecca had gotten a call from Hoyt. Guy Ragsdill had died from his injuries.

"You keep calling the man my nephew. Which one?"

It was a bluff.

"Lewis. Edmond's oldest son." She pulled a picture of the young man from the file. "I thought family meant something to you mafia wannabe types. Guess not. You took advantage of your father's death to start a new life, then killed your brother and nephew." She pulled a postmortem picture of Lewis from the file. "Bashed his face in with a rock. That's cold."

Smith didn't flinch from the image. "Like I said, I was only defending myself."

"Why would he attack you? Did he know that you killed his father out at sea?" She paused and let the silence stretch.

When Chase didn't respond this time, she tried a different strategy. "How did you manage to get Edmond to work with you when he wanted out of the life so much?"

Chase only smirked. "I don't know what you're talking about."

"I think you do. Your brother wanted out of the life, and—"

"My brother was a pussy."

"And managed to stay out of the life until your father's death. From that moment on, though, you dragged him back. How?"

Chase spread his hands as far as he could manage. "Still don't know what you mean."

Rebecca took a breath. She needed to lean into his narcissism. Needed to lean into his compulsion to win.

"I'm wondering if Edmond got sick of following orders and decided to take over the business himself. With you officially dead, he did hold all the cards, didn't he? He could turn on you in a second. How did it feel, knowing your little brother had such power over you?"

The table shook as Chase attempted to stand, and Rebecca shot a look at Darian, silently telling him to stay back. Her deputy's mouth was set in a hard line, but he didn't interfere.

"My little brother held nothing over me."

She laughed. "I call bullshit. That's why you killed him. Because you'd finally had enough of following his orders."

She had no idea if she was right, but it didn't matter. All that mattered was pissing Smith off so much he spoke without thinking.

"He was robbing me! I..." His eyes widened as he realized his mistake. He grew still.

"Was Skipper stealing from you too?"

Silence.

"And Lewis?"

Silence.

That was okay. Though Rebecca might not yet know where each piece of the puzzle fit, she would soon enough.

"I want to see my lawyer now."

Rebecca shut her file folder with a satisfied snap and stood. "Of course."

That was fine with her. The admission was enough, and she had no doubt that others would follow. None of it felt particularly good, though.

She still had to call Wanda Chase and tell her that she found her son. He was in the same place as her husband now.

"What's an eleven-letter word for mighty matriarch? It has to end with R."

Rebecca looked up from the update she'd been reading to find Hoyt at her door, newspaper in hand.

"Grandmother."

"Dammit. I hate when I'm stupid."

The deputy wrote down his answer. Before he walked back down the hallway, she turned her monitor to face him. "He confessed on all counts."

Hoyt lowered the newspaper and came into the office. "I'll be damned."

Rebecca grinned, wishing she'd been the one to squeeze the confession out of Marcus Chase, but satisfied that she'd given the Feds something to work with.

When he'd finished reading about how Chase had murdered Edmond because he'd been skimming from the profits, Hoyt took a seat.

"I *will* be damned. You're right. Skipper was collateral damage, and Mac…um, Lewis, had come here to track him down."

"That young man never stood a chance in that family."

Hoyt nodded. "Sad but true." He grabbed his newspaper and stood.

Rebecca noticed the headline "Shadow Island Preservation Society Meets Today."

She'd heard the rumors about the organization wanting to remodel the Noble Lighthouse, a significant landmark.

It was the renaming of the building that was causing the controversy. Most folks wanted it to stay the way it was to preserve its historical significance. Ironically, it was the Preservation Society that wanted to make the change.

"It's a nice day when all we have to worry about is town gossip and infighting, isn't it?"

"What?" Hoyt looked up from where he was entering something new in his puzzle and raised an eyebrow. She pointed at the headline facing her.

She attempted to read the upside-down article. *"The historical society is warning that, after a recent structural survey, the lighthouse is on the brink of collapse."*

Hoyt shook out the paper and angled it to read the article himself. "What the hell does changing the lighthouse name have to do with raising money to save it?"

Rebecca snatched the paper from his hands. "I have no idea." She went back to the front page where a huge picture of the lighthouse took center stage. "I used to love staring up at that thing as a kid."

Hoyt grinned. "Me too. We used to dare each other to climb to the top. It's still got a spiral staircase inside, but the windows blew out, so it's all rusted. About the only person who could safely go up those stairs was a kid. I doubt they'd hold even that little bit of weight now."

"Sheriff?" Viviane popped her head around the corner of the door. "We've got a disturbing-the-peace call."

Rebecca sighed. The call was disturbing *her* peace.

"Where is it?"

"It's at the old Alton place."

Hoyt's head snapped up. "The old Alton place? Who the hell would be causing a ruckus all the way out there?"

"It's Mason Alton. He's back in town."

The End
To be continued...

Thank you for reading.
All of the *Shadow Island Series* books can be found on Amazon.

ACKNOWLEDGMENTS

How does one properly thank everyone involved in taking a dream and making it a reality? Here goes.

In addition to our families, whose unending support provided the foundation for us to find the time and energy to put these thoughts on paper, we want to thank the editors who polished our words and made them shine.

Many thanks to our publisher for risking taking on two newbies and giving us the confidence to become bona fide authors.

More than anyone, we want to thank you, our readers, for sharing your most important asset, your time, with this book. We hope with all our hearts we made it worthwhile.

Much love,
Mary & Lori

ACKNOWLEDGMENTS

ABOUT THE AUTHOR

Mary Stone

Mary Stone lives among the majestic Blue Ridge Mountains of East Tennessee with her two dogs, four cats, a couple of energetic boys, and a very patient husband.

As a young girl, she would go to bed every night, wondering what type of creature might be lurking underneath. It wasn't until she was older that she learned that the creatures she needed to most fear were human.

Today, she creates vivid stories with courageous, strong heroines and dastardly villains. She invites you to enter her world of serial killers, FBI agents but never damsels in distress. Her female characters can handle themselves, going toe-to-toe with any male character, protagonist or antagonist.

Discover more about Mary Stone on her website.
www.authormarystone.com

Lori Rhodes

As a tiny girl, from the moment Lori Rhodes first dipped her toe into the surf on a barrier island of Virginia, she was in love. When she grew up and learned all the deep, dark secrets and horrible acts people could commit against each other, she couldn't stop the stories from coming out of the other end of her pen. Somehow, her magical island and the darkness got mixed together and ended up in her first novel. Now, she spends her days making sure the guests at her beach rental cottages are happy, and her nights dreaming up the characters who love her island as much as she does.

Connect with Mary Online

facebook.com/authormarystone
twitter.com/MaryStoneAuthor
goodreads.com/AuthorMaryStone
bookbub.com/profile/3378576590
pinterest.com/MaryStoneAuthor
instagram.com/marystoneauthor
tiktok.com/@authormarystone

Made in the USA
Las Vegas, NV
26 September 2024

95812991R00144